W9-CAY-415

the
Chance
to Fly

the
Chance

to Fly

by Tony Award winner

ALI STROKER & STACY DAVIDOWITZ

AMULET BOOKS
NEW YORK

Cataloging-in-Publication Data has been applied for and may be obtained from the Library of Congress.

ISBN 978-1-4197-4393-1

Book design by Marcie Lawrence

Printed and bound in U.S.A.
10 9 8 7 6 5 4 3 2 1

ABRAMS The Art of Books
195 Broadway, New York, NY 10007
abramsbooks.com

For every kid who has a dream, even if the odds are against you, don't ever stop finding ways to fly.

CHAPTER ONE

A House Is Not a Home

"I FOUND OKLAHOMA!" Nat screamed from the back seat of her family's Nissan Altima, jolting her dad awake from the passenger seat. She snapped a photo of the license plate.

"That's a point, Natty baby," her mom said, drumming on the steering wheel.

"Are you *sure*?" Nat replied, then burst into song. "*YOU'RE DOING FINE, OKLAHOMA*—"

Her mom smirked at her through the rearview mirror. "All right, hotshot."

The Beacon family was dominating the License Plate Game. They'd been playing for six days straight, but with a twist—spotting plates from states where famous musicals were set got double the points. Nat's spotting of the Oklahoma plate had pushed her family's total score over thirty, and so, as they'd discussed, they'd reward themselves with dessert for dinner! Nat would definitely have to remind her parents about that.

"Hon, you're drooling," Nat's mom said.

"Me or Warbucks?" Nat's dad asked groggily.

At the mention of his name, Warbucks leaped from Nat's lap into her dad's lap and back. Nat lowered the window so he could stick his big floppy head out, but the stench of manure filled the car. Warbucks wasn't the *smartest* of service dogs—he'd flunked out when he couldn't retain commands past *sit* and *get*—but he was smart enough to hide from the smell of New Jersey meadowland. He plopped onto the floor, a Labradoodle fluff mountain beneath Nat's feet, and chewed his California Raisin toy. Like Nat, he was forever loyal to his home state.

With the window back up, the Beach Boys played on full blast. Nat groaned as her dad broke into a shoulder shimmy. "Oh, come on, Natty! What are you ashamed of? It's just us!"

It wasn't that she was ashamed. It was that the song, "California Girls," was flooding her with all the feels. It made her think of the summers she'd spent back home, at the beach with her best friend and soul sister, Chloe, as they navigated the sand like action heroes. As they read juicy teen celebrity buzz in *Popstar!* magazine and took every love quiz under the sun. She knew the song was supposed to be about hot girls, the kind who splash around in the shallow water and attract random photoshoots, not misfits who attract unnecessary lifeguard rescues. But still. They were California girls. It was the start of summer. The lyrics made her homesick.

"*Hamilton*, anyone?" Nat piped up.

Now it was her mom who groaned.

Nat protested, "How else am I going to prepare for my future groundbreaking performance as Eliza Schuyler Hamilton?"

In their big cross-country move, they'd listened to the entire Broadway cast recording, and the *Mixtape*, and the deleted songs—twice per day, every day. When Nat sang along, she'd sink into Eliza's shoes. Imagine Eliza's problems were her own and that her own problems were gone. Time would melt into meters of music. And when the soundtrack was complete, Nat would snap back into herself, already craving another escape.

Like now.

Nat's mom exhaled like a deflating balloon. "Sweetie, can we just relax for a little? When you belt along, the energy becomes very . . . charged."

"What if I don't belt? What if I use my head voice, and we listen to, like, *Les Miz* or *Phantom*?"

"Natalie, we don't have that much longer to go."

"Pleeeease! I should practice. One day, the perfect show for me is going to come along."

"*Maaaybe*," her mom said with so much doubt that she might as well have said "Never." She tried to clarify, "I just have no idea how theater works and how it would work for you . . ."

"When I was your age, I also had big dreams," her dad cut in. "I was determined to be the next Michael Jordan!"

Nat couldn't help but take that as an insult. "I don't want to be the next *anyone*," she explained. "I want people to want to be the next me."

Her dad forced a smile. "Well, good news. You've had years of racing training, and it's just starting to pay off."

"On the track, you shine," her mom added. "Don't you think so, Jeff?"

"I know so. A star in the making."

Nat wasn't delusional. She understood why her dreams of becoming an actress made her parents shut down—they loved her and didn't want to see her get hurt. At the end of the day, who would give a kid like her a shot? With all the talented girls out there, who would look outside the box and choose her? So far, no one. But that was because Nat had never auditioned for a play before. She'd gotten to sing in her school's chorus concerts, but there she wasn't stepping into a character's shoes and making unique acting choices or anything. Her job was to blend.

"Anyway, I'm gonna close my eyes again," Nat's dad went on. "So if you must listen to musical theater, maybe use your headphones?"

Nat would have agreed, but her mom had unknowingly put her headphones through the laundry. One ear sounded tinny, and the other sounded like the artist was singing underwater.

She hadn't told her parents yet. She didn't need them thinking she was more dependent than they already thought she was.

"Why don't you look for a Maine license plate?" Nat's mom suggested. "Or South Carolina? Isn't there a musical that takes place in the Carolinas?"

"Are you thinking of *Caroline, or Change*?" Nat asked. "Because that takes place in Louisiana."

"Louisiana, then."

Nat sighed, then rested her temple on the car door. She gazed out the window at the blur of trees—maybe pine, definitely not palm—as an NPR ad for Metamucil fiber supplements depressingly droned on the radio. She imagined the ad playing out like one of her favorite scenes from *Annie*—with the radio show and the Boylan Sisters and the APPLAUSE sign cueing the audience to cheer—and that made listening more bearable.

Annie had been Nat's introduction to musicals. Chloe's parents had taken them to see a community theater production of it when they were seven. Chloe had thought the show was okay slash kind of boring. But Nat had been mesmerized. She'd teared up when the orphans sang about their fantasy parents during "Maybe." She'd felt her stomach coil when Miss Hannigan, the evil head of the orphanage, sang "Little Girls." And then, at the end, when Annie got adopted, Nat had to hug herself to contain her happiness. After that, Nat wanted to learn about every musical there was.

Before Nat could choose between a nap and finding a Louisiana license plate, a call from Chloe Suarez erupted through the speakers. Nat cried out to her as if they hadn't spoken in a decade. "CHLOEEEEEE?"

"Nat? Omigod, I have to tell you the most embarrassing thing. I was in CVS, buying laxative gummies—"

"You're on speaker, Chloe. Sorry—my Bluetooth is still connected."

Chloe paused, her silence echoing around the car.

"*Hi, Chlo-Chlo,*" Nat's mom and dad spoke-sang together.

Nat's eyes bulged. She and Chloe were used to her parents being *involved*, but that didn't mean they wanted to blab about embarrassing stuff with them. They were thirteen, not nine. Chloe gulped, clearly feeling the same. "Hi, Mandy. Hi, Jeff. Hi, Warbucks." Warbucks began unhelpfully licking the dashboard, making Chloe's voice cut in and out. "So, how—longer till—get there?"

"We've got about forty minutes," Nat's mom replied.

"Forty minutes?!" Nat asked, her head spinning.

"Are you excited?" Chloe asked. "You sound excited."

"Yes," Nat's parents said.

"No," Nat overlapped.

"Cooooool," Chloe said. "Well, your new job as an *actionary* sounds like a good opportunity, Mandy."

"It's called an *actuary*," Nat corrected. "And it's just hard math."

"It's not *just* hard math," Nat's mom protested. "I also measure risk. If you're looking for someone to tell you the worst-case scenario, I'm your gal!"

"Ha! Okay!" Chloe said.

Nat wished Chloe wasn't so polite to her parents. If the roles were reversed and Chloe's parents were whisking her away across the country for forever, all so her mom could take on the most uncreative job in the universe, Nat would stand up for her best friend, not compliment Chloe's mom and then mistake Chloe's obvious dread for excitement.

"I think this is the longest we've ever been separate," Nat blurted, cutting her dad off as he excitedly explained *his* new job as the athletics director at Saddle Stream High School.

"I think so, too," Chloe said.

Nat felt a lump in the back of her throat. She and Chloe had been inseparable since nursery school—ever since Josh B. had called them alien twins. They'd cried apart, then laughed about it together, then made friendship bracelets out of shoelaces dipped in neon-green paint, then convinced Josh B. that they *were*, in fact, alien twins, and things had only gotten weirder, tighter, funnier, best friend–ier from there. No one understood her like Chloe, and no one understood Chloe like Nat. "I'll miss you every day, my alien," Nat managed to croak.

"Aw, me too. But don't worry, it's not going to be that bad," Chloe said.

hat?! Had they been talking in private, Nat would have ed, "OF COURSE IT'LL BE THAT BAD!" But she didn't want extra coddling from her parents, so instead she asked, "We'll Skype later?"

"Yeah, always," Chloe said. "Also, Natty's not gonna say it, but she needs new headphones!"

"Chlo!"

"What's wrong with your headphones?" Nat's mom asked her.

Nat winced. "I left them in my pocket, and you washed them."

"Nat! Why didn't you—" Nat's mom tossed her arms up. "Chloe, this is why we need you!" She pointed to her purse at Nat's dad's feet. "Jeff, can you grab my wireless headphones? Nat, sweetie, give your dad your phone. He'll connect them for you."

"It's okay. I know how Bluetooth works."

"It's not a problem, hon. It's just me being a parent."

That was Nat's mom's excuse for everything: Nat, I'll take your plate. Nat, what time did you want your alarm set? Nat, let me pick out your random classmate's birthday present. *It's not a problem. It's just me being a parent.* Nat reluctantly gave her phone over to her dad.

"And Chloe out," Chloe said. "Bye, Beacons. Bye, Nat Cat."

"Love ya, Chlo," Nat said.

With Chloe suddenly gone, the car air felt stale. Nat couldn't help but wonder why her best friend didn't care more that she'd moved. Nat's dad gave her the phone back, but the connected headphones were uncharged and beeping to death.

Nat noticed her parents' hands clasped together, fingers in a tight white-knuckle grip over the empty cup holder. She felt like she should say sorry to them but also that they should say sorry to her—for what, exactly, she wasn't sure. She waited for her dad to turn back on NPR, but to her happy surprise, he threw on "The Schuyler Sisters" instead.

Nat pressed her forehead against the window as her family peeled off the highway. WELCOME TO SADDLE STREAM, a weathered wooden sign read. Saddled horses and streams were a nice thought, but a Google search had taught her that the name was misleading—the town had no saddled horses or streams. Though, apparently, it had a decent-sized shopping mall, with a carousel and a fountain. The town's namers were clearly aspiring toward charm, and, hey, Nat couldn't blame anyone for an aspiration.

"In an eighth of a mile, turn right onto— Turn right onto Cherry Brook Lane."

"Is this our block?" Nat asked, taking in the sudden stretch of big, short homes. "The houses look kind of weird, like they're squatting."

"They're ranches—only one level," Nat's mom explained. "Perfectly stunning, perfectly perfect for us!"

"You just said 'perfect' a lot of times," Nat told her.

"You have arrived at your destination."

Nat's chest tightened as they pulled into a "ranch" with *1224* in tacky gold lettering above the garage door. She'd half expected the house to be a replica of her home in San Francisco, sitting on top of a winding hill with two lemon trees hugging the driveway. But there was no hill, and there were no lemon trees. Just a sloped lawn lined with white-barked trees that were peeling like dead skin after a sunburn.

"And . . . we are here!" Nat's dad cheered, circling his fist in the air. As he lowered his arm, Nat spotted a ramp. An extremely long inclined monster of a ramp that connected the driveway to the stoop at, like, a 45-degree angle.

"Ah! Natty, let's get you out of there," her mom said, rushing to the trunk. As Nat listened to her parents assemble her wheelchair named Peaches by putting the wheels onto the frame, she decided she wouldn't take off her seat belt. She would stay in the car and convince her parents to drive back to California, where there was an easy, accessible entrance into the house through the garage and literally everything was better.

"You want to unbuckle?" her dad asked, arriving at the back seat.

Nat unbuckled with a silent sigh of dread and put her arms out. Her dad reached in, his arms under her pits, and lifted her out of the car and into her chair. Starved of play, Warbucks leaped out of the car, raced across the lawn, and pawed at a swarm of gnats. The sun was setting behind the house, wrapping it in a pink cotton-candy ribbon. It was grossly pretty. Nat had never been so nostalgic for Bay Area smog.

"I had the movers set up and arrange all the big stuff this week!" her mom said, clapping with glee. "Want the tour?" Before Nat could obediently nod, her mom was holding her hand and bringing her to the ramp. She guided Nat over the lip of wood and then started to pull her up.

Nat could suddenly hear kids biking past their house—clanking chains, skidding tires, snickering. She refused to look behind her. Instead, she shrunk into her chair, reliving the humiliating time last year when her mom had pulled her up a ramp to the auditorium stage to accept her honor roll certificate. In the longest thirty seconds of her life, she'd tried not to cry as a row of eighth-grade girls had exploded with giggles. The last thing she wanted now was to have possible new friends watch her get dragged into her own house by her mom. "I can do it," Nat insisted, wriggling her hand free to grip the wheels.

"I don't know, sweetie. It's kind of steep."

"I'll try it from the bottom of the ramp."

Nat rolled a little backward with her dad in a lunge behind her, his palms an inch from her back. She gripped the wheels again, and with a deep breath, she *puuushed*. Halfway up, her stomach knotted, and her arms felt like Jell-O.

Her dad cheered her on. "Think of it as training for racing!"

Her mom broke into an actual cheer: "*Nat-a-WE BELIEVE IN YA!*"

Nat believed in herself. But she also believed entering her promised "totally accessible" house should be *easy*. Not a Paralympic workout.

About three-quarters of the way up, Nat hit a wall. Her fingers were burning against the wheels, and she wasn't going up or down. As she stalled, her mom's voice vibrated like a rubber band. "Jeff, you got her?" That was all the motivation Nat needed. She worked through the pain in her gut, fingers, and arms, and *wheeeeeeeled!* Without any help, she was only a foot from the top and steadily climbing, when her DAD PUSHED HER up onto the stoop. She'd been *so close*.

"Well, that was— I'm impressed!" Nat's mom said.

"Someone's ready to race again!" her dad added. "What do *you* think?"

I think a house isn't a home if I can't get inside of it. "Yeah, that—was—hard," Nat panted instead. She glanced behind her to the street. Not a bike, not a sound. Before the relief could set in, her mom was guiding her inside for a tour.

The kitchen countertops were low enough that she could reach the appliances on them, unlike the countertops in their California kitchen. The dining room walls were painted "Quiet Time," which was gray, and the living room walls were painted "Soft Focus," which was a blander shade of gray. According to her mom, Nat shouldn't mind the worn-in couches and rugs from back home—her only sense of comfort in this strange place—because they'd be put to the curb as soon as the new furniture arrived.

"It's amazing, huh?" her mom asked on the way to Nat's bedroom.

Nat forced a smile. She missed everything about her old house—the burnt-orange paint and the wheel-tracked carpet and the broken doorbell that sang "Happy Birthday." She just hoped she liked her room. She'd helped pick out the colors and the Paint and Petals bedding from Anthropologie, but she wasn't sure how it was all going to come together.

Her dad pretended to press a fob to her door and then dramatically kicked it open. "Jeff!" her mom shouted. "You've left a footmark!"

The room was huge. The bed, with its smooth floral comforter, looked like the icing of a Sam's Club sheet cake. Framed inspirational posters—THE WORLD IS YOUR OYSTER and NEVER EVER GIVE UP and SHOOT FOR THE MOON; EVEN IF YOU MISS, YOU'LL LAND AMONG THE STARS—were propped against lavender walls. Once they were hung up, Nat was pretty sure her room would have the same vibe as her old therapist's waiting room.

"It's so *you*, right, Nat?" her mom asked, running her fingers along one of the frames.

"Totally." The cheesy quotes were so her mom, but that's not to say Nat didn't like them. They were like pretty pep talks that made her heart bounce when she read them at the right times.

Nat was pushing toward her desk when she caught a glimpse of herself in the closet-door mirror. She looked tired. And awkward—her upper body strong and built, and her legs small and thin. Nat had never seen any girls her age with a body like her own. Being paralyzed made it uniquely hers. She sometimes tried to picture what she'd look like if she weren't in a wheelchair, but after a lot of mental gymnastics, her brain could never land on legs that matched her body. Nat could only ever see herself as she was.

"Wait till you see this," her mom said, pushing open a second door. It was a roomy made-for-her bathroom with stylish pink-and-white-checkered tiles, a roll-in shower, and . . . another door. "Like back home," her mom said, slowly opening it to reveal—voilà!—the master bedroom.

Nat was hearing warning sirens. *ATTENTION: Your rooms are CONNECTED through a SHARED BATHROOM. There is a thing called PRIVACY you will never have!*

"What do you think?" her dad asked, giving the space an air hug.

"It's, uh, it's cool," Nat said. She'd loved the convenience of having a connecting room until about two years ago, when she and Chloe had started their Friday night sleepovers. They'd be talking about private things, like celebrity crushes and body stuff, when they'd hear Nat's dad putting the toilet seat up and peeing.

Nat's mom could clearly tell Nat wasn't actually digging the house. She sighed, then sat on the edge of Nat's bed. "This move is *a lot*, Natty, we know. With connecting rooms, though, we're right here if you need us. It's a simple way to ease the transition."

"*Riiight*," Nat said. "But, like, the rooms will stay connected even after the transition?"

"Correct," Nat's mom said.

Nat felt her nose stuff up with the new house smell. Of course she understood where her mom was coming from. She'd always need help with stuff like getting in and out of the car and opening and wheeling through manual doors. But extra help seemed out of place. Her Wheel Friends were starting to have "independence talks" with their parents, where they went over things that they could try to do on their own, and this felt like the opposite of that.

"It's okay to get help," Nat's mom said. "We want to help you."

"We like helping you," her dad said. "Love it!"

Help, help, help. If she heard that word one more time, she might scream.

Nat's dad gave her a kiss on her temple. "Hey, let's get out of here, huh?"

"Jeff, we *just* got here," her mom said. "I think we're all a bit tired."

He bumped his eyebrows. "Too tired for pie?"

Nat had totally forgotten. "THE LICENSE PLATE GAME! WE GET DESSERT FOR DINNER!"

That apparently cued Warbucks, who charged into the room and shook out short blades of grass from his fur.

"Noooooo," Nat's mom groaned.

"I need to get out of these car clothes," Nat mumbled, already rummaging through her duffel. Her mom stood up, eager to help her pick out her outfit, but Nat was quick to find what she needed. She threw her chosen clothes on the bed and the bag on the floor, then pushed open the bathroom door. For her parents.

"Gimme two minutes," she told them. "I'll meet you by the front door."

She began shoving on her favorite ripped jeans in true Nat fashion: putting each foot in the correct pant leg, pulling the jeans up to her thighs, and then inching each side up a tug at a time. She reapplied her vanilla deodorant, threw on her tie-dye zip-up, and rolled out, rallying for sugar.

CHAPTER TWO

There Are Worse Things I Could Do

"Hiya there, Oakley!" Nat said, putting on her best Wild West accent to greet her lime-green racing wheelchair.

In the humid, blazing parking lot of Redker's College, her dad pumped the perfect amount of air into the chair's third wheel. "What is that—Australian?" he asked. "Aren't the Oakley sunglasses headquarters in California?"

"What? You think I named Oakley 'Oakley' after sunglasses?"

"What are *those*?" he asked, pointing at her shades.

"They're Ray-Bans," she replied flatly. "I named Oakley after *Annie* Oakley." Blank stare. "*Annie Get Your Gun*." Another blank stare. "It's, like, a world-famous *musical*."

"Ah! A *musical*," her dad joked, as if he'd only just learned what one was. He helped her transfer from Peaches to Oakley, which was perfectly custom-fitted to her body, and she snapped on her matching lime-green-and-purple-flowered helmet. "So, you ready to sign up for the Lightning Wheels?" he asked.

"Sure, yeah."

"That's it? *Sure, yeah*?" He inhaled with drama. "I said, 'ARE YOU READY TO REGISTER AND GET SOME DAD-DAUGHTER PRACTICING IN BEFORE YOU MEET THE TEAM TOMORROW, SO HELP ME GOD?' "

"Ready!" Nat shouted with a giggle. She raced after him as he high-kneed it toward the track. Three painfully boring days of Netflix, cereal, and unpacking had passed, and she was honestly just excited to have a reason to get out of the house. She crossed her gloved fingers that the Lightning Wheels would be just like the Zoomers, the team she'd dedicated three years to back home. She and her Wheel Friends had had as much fun off the track as they did on, especially during out-of-state competitions, like the Junior Paralympics in Denver, Colorado, where they'd had wild sleepover parties in hotel rooms and ordered "cheeseburgers with every cheese" via room service.

"Hey, hey, I'm Cynthia—the coach."

Nat's eyes followed the raspy smoker's voice to a white woman with frizzy gray hair that was pulled back in a scrunchie. Cynthia waddled over to the gate's entrance, which was odd in and of itself—Serena, her Zoomers coach, was in a chair, which was how she understood how to coach *wheelchair racing*. "You must be Natalie."

"Yeah, hi," Nat said. "It's nice to meet you."

"Yup, same," Cynthia said. She then looked at Nat's dad, who had his fist out for a bump. "And you must be *Jeff*." She bumped him back but said his name like it was dripping with nasty protein powder.

"Great meeting you in person!" Nat's dad said, seemingly unfazed. They moved to the track. "I appreciate you letting me chat your ear off last night."

"Uh-huh."

"I really wanted you to get a sense of Nat's stats and also what a great kid she is. From one coach to another, I think you'll find she's going to be an awesome addition to the team."

Cynthia moved a loose whistle around in her palm like a stress ball, but Nat was the one feeling stressed. Knowing her dad, he'd probably bragged about how she'd been awarded lots of medals, leaving out the fact that she'd gotten sixth place *one time* and that the rest of her awards were for stuff like Sportsmanship and Most Improved.

"I'm looking forward to seeing what you've got, Natalie," Cynthia said. "But I'm not gonna lie—we've been training for the new season since the late spring. You're gonna have to play catch-up." She knocked on Nat's helmet.

"Oh, ha," Nat mumbled. She watched her dad's Adam's apple slide up and down so hard it looked like it might pop out through his neck.

Cynthia pointed to Nat's compensator, which was basically a steering lever that made the chair go straight or hold a curve around the track. "Why don't you set that—"

"Already set!" Nat's dad cut in way too enthusiastically.

"Why don't you *test* it," she said to Nat. "And take a few warm-up laps while your dad and I get your registration in order."

"Nat can absolutely do that," her dad said. "She is one hundred percent up for any challenge."

"All right, Jeff. Follow me to my office. Natalie, we'll meet you back out here in ten."

"Cool, okay," Nat said, disappointed. The Zoomers had welcomed her to the team with a T-shirt, pink wristbands, and a cheer: "*What's the boom? ZOOM, ZOOM! What's the boom? ZOOM, ZOOM!*" And they'd celebrated her dad's involvement, not treated him like the annoying kid in class who the teacher can't stand.

She bravely pushed to the starting line, threw in her mom's wireless headphones, and pressed shuffle on her Broadway playlist. "Memory" from *Cats* blasted into her ears—probably the saddest, loneliest, pump-down song on the mix. Nat fumbled with her headphones to change the track and took off to the sound of violins, her compensator set to straight. It wasn't until she was approaching the curve and a chorus of dead people started singing that she realized she was listening to the finale of *Titanic*—*definitely* the saddest, loneliest, pump-down song on the mix. She stopped, and four college-age students in matching maroon uniforms sprinted past her, then cut back into her lane.

"Sorr—" she started to say. But they were already a few paces ahead. She swallowed her needless apology and checked her phone. 10:13 AM. Six minutes had felt like twenty. She struck the compensator, ripped the headphones from her ears, and wheeled off the track and into the sports facility building to find her dad.

As the automatic doors opened, Nat felt a blast of AC that sent her arm hair straight up. The lobby was unexpectedly beautiful. Its high walls were covered with old-school windows. Strong summer light streamed in, casting a racing chair shadow across the marble floor. She spotted what could have been an office door across the lobby and rolled toward it, passing an old telephone booth, a closed-up box office, and next to that, double wooden doors, one of which was slightly open. Nat rolled past the doorway and caught a glimpse of red. Curious, she stopped. She wheeled back and peeked inside. It was a theater.

Nat's heart instantly sped up. Without thinking, she went inside. There were fifty to sixty raked seats in front of a stage covered by a classic red velvet curtain. The space looked dusty, abandoned almost, except for a bulletin board on the side wall littered with flyers. They were mostly dull ads for stuff like tutoring, laptop fixer-uppers, cat sitters, and apartment rentals. But bordering the notices was a series of hot-pink and green papers—the opposite of dull. She inched closer to read what they said.

CALLING ALL KIDS 10–13 YEARS OLD . . .

AUDITION FOR BROADWAY BOUNDERS'
SUMMER PRODUCTION OF

WICKED

SUNDAY, JUNE 28TH—10 AM TO 1 PM
AT THE JCC IN SADDLE STREAM, NJ

(ACROSS FROM REDKER'S COLLEGE SPORTS FACILITY)

REHEARSALS AND PERFORMANCES
RUN A TOTAL OF 4 WEEKS!

She read it again. And again. But her jitters made the words bob around in her brain, their meaning just . . . not . . . sinking in. She snagged the bottommost flyer, and as she stared at it in her trembling hands, everything started to make sense. There were auditions tomorrow. For a musical. But not just *any* musical. *Wicked*. Her second favorite to *Hamilton*. Hey, maybe even tied for first.

Everything she knew about the show danced in her head all at once. *Wicked* was the prequel to *The Wizard of Oz*, the untold story of the witches. There was Elphaba—a talented, fiery, misunderstood young woman born with emerald skin. And then there was Glinda—a bubbly blond. They were rivals, then friends, oh my! And in the end, the world decided to call one Wicked and the other Good. It was amazing.

Nat had never seen the show. Before she was born and before it had transferred to Broadway, it had premiered at San Francisco's Curran Theatre, and even though there had been other West Coast productions since, they usually conflicted with racing and her mom's late work schedule. That hadn't stopped her from listening to the original Broadway cast recording on repeat since birth, though. "Defying Gravity" had been her ringtone for the last two years. She knew the lyrics to practically every song. She also knew that another one of the witches, Elphaba's sister, Nessarose, was in a wheelchair.

Nessarose wasn't a witch to be overlooked. Mistook to be meek and quiet, she was actually a diva on wheels with a wicked-sweet crush and wicked-savvy dreams. She was yearning for love. Yearning to be accepted. Yearning to feel normal.

It was a part made just for her.

Forget racing. Nat was already there, onstage at the JCC, making her biggest dream of all come true.

CHAPTER THREE

My Shot

"I don't know," Nat's dad said at dinner, stabbing his fork into chickpea pasta. "Mandy, back me up."

"I am," she answered through a mouthful of steamed broccoli. "I agree."

"You agree with—with what?" Nat tripped with panic.

Her dad pointed at her glass of milk and chewed the pasta left in his mouth. Nat waited, trying to prepare a counter to whatever glass-half-full analogy he was about to make. But when he swallowed, all he said was "Nat, if you're not going to eat your pasta, please drink up."

Nat did everything in her power not to freak out. No, she would not be lathering her throat with dairy—known enemy to vocal cords—less than fifteen hours before an audition. She'd sooner drink Warbucks's water, with its floating chunks of soggy dog food, because at least that wouldn't make her voice CRACK.

Nat took a deep, don't-blow-this breath. After she'd found the flyer, she'd rolled back outside and listened to the *Wicked* soundtrack until her dad had come out for practice. Lap after lap, he'd whooped encouragement as she raced, the possibility of being in the musical sparking an electric current through her body. She'd zipped around the track with scary speed, and she and her dad had left Redker's flying high for totally different reasons.

Thirty seconds into dinner, Nat had spilled the truth. She would not be going to the first wheelchair-racing practice tomorrow. She would be going across the street to the JCC, where she'd be auditioning for her very first and favorite and forever-in-love-with musical, *Wicked.* That cool?

Apparently not.

"Look, Nat," her dad went on, prying his eyes from her untouched milk. "It's unfair to the Lightning Wheels, who are expecting you to show up and be a part of their team. Coach Cynthia seems great."

Nat gave him side-eye.

"Fine, not *great.* But tough. If you ditch tomorrow's practice to audition for some musical, Cynthia might not look past that."

"It's not just *some musical,*" Nat insisted, pressing her palms onto the table to keep her frustration from flapping out of her fingers. "It's *Wicked.*"

Nat's dad blew out a sigh, and with it, a chunk of boiled carrot. "Okay, say theoretically you get into the show—"

"If I get in, I'll quit racing." She'd delivered a heart-stab. She watched guiltily as her dad's face matched the color of the lone beet on his plate. "For now, I mean," she rushed to add. "I can rejoin in the fall."

"If Cynthia lets you," he said. "The rehearsals and the show—how long is it?"

"Four weeks."

"You'd give up years of racing training for a month of drama?"

A high, wailing YES. "I think so?"

Nat's dad stood up, then sat back down and wrung his hands out even though they weren't wet. His meltdown kind of made sense to Nat—he'd invested a lot of time and money into her racing career—but still, he was being *dramatic.*

"Jeff, breathe," Nat's mom murmured. "Nat, sweetie. We just moved here. Racing is a fantastic and easy way to make friends."

"So is doing a show."

Nat watched her mom stop herself from saying it. Then it slipped out anyway. "I mean friends who are, you know, in the same position as you."

"You mean in a wheelchair?"

"C'mon, honey, that's not what I— Well, it is, but—" Nat's mom's hand blanketed Nat's against the table. "Connecting with brave, athletic young people with whom you share so much in common—it's a beautiful thing."

"I've never had friends who love theater like I do."

Nat's mom shut her eyes for a long second, and Nat could see her words twitching behind her pursed lips. "Is there a part that's right for you? I mean, just—realistically?"

Nat lit up as she delivered the news she'd been saving. "Yeah, there's a part for a girl just like me: Nessarose. She's the sister of the Wicked Witch of the West, and she's IN A WHEELCHAIR!!!" Mic drop. Nat pulled her hand out from underneath her mom's. "It's perfect, right?! There's no other musical I can think of where they ACTUALLY NEED ME!"

Her parents STILL seemed unconvinced. "Right . . ." her mom said.

"Huh," her dad overlapped. "But how are you going to stay active doing a play?"

Nat shook her head in disbelief. "Um, *dancing.*" She was met with a hollow stare. "I can dance. People in chairs can—I've told you about the Rollettes, Dad." She looked at her mom for backup. "I've told you both about them and how they're an incredible dance team of girls in wheelchairs. Like, I've talked about them a lot. A *lot.*"

"Right, right, I remember," her dad said, massaging his own shoulders. "Maybe if there was a local Rollettes team, that would be a good thing to do alongside racing."

"What?!" There was no local Rollettes team. There was one Rollettes team based in LA, and the girls were more like young women in their twenties. If he'd listened to her when she'd talked about anything other than racing, he'd have known that. "That's not even the point," Nat asserted, her frustration now pumping through her veins. "The point is: I can dance in *Wicked* because there's a role for me."

Again, her logic fell flat. "What if the one role you think you're right for has already been cast?" her mom asked.

"By another actress in a wheelchair?!"

"By anyone," her mom replied. "Do you even know if the space is accessible?"

No. "The JCC website says they have an elevator . . ."

"I don't know why you're not giving racing a chance," Nat's mom pressed. "We both know how much you love it—"

"I love theater more," Nat argued, her anger suddenly bubbling up to her throat.

"How do you *know* that?" her dad asked.

"I JUST DO!"

Nat's dad leaned in to tuck one of Nat's dirty-blond curls behind her ear, and just that little bit of contact made her chin turn into a mini earthquake. He spoke gently. "Natty. In racing, you belong. Not just belong, you *excel*."

Her mom leaned in, holding Nat's chin. "You've built up this whole show experience based on a single flyer, hon. It's hard enough being the new kid. We just don't want you getting hurt. Or feeling disappointed. Does that make sense?"

It kind of did, but it mostly didn't. Her parents weren't listening. They didn't get it. Just today her dad had left her ALONE on the track. So why couldn't he leave her with A LOT OF PEOPLE in a theater? Nat's heart thundered with defeat, and the tears began spilling down her cheeks. She wanted to slap herself. How could she expect her parents to treat her like an independent, mature person when she couldn't even talk to them without crying like a baby?!

Back in her bedroom and all cried out, Nat pulled the *Annie* program from her bookshelf and flipped through the bios of the orphans. They were all sorts of different kids. Different ages, different looks, different theater credits. Some liked school, some gave shout-outs to sports teams, some thanked God. If they could follow their dreams, why couldn't she? Nat's brain started plotting hard and fast, ideas ramming into one another, fusing together, crystalizing. If her parents wouldn't take her to the JCC, she'd just have to take herself.

CHAPTER FOUR

Bring It On

Nat waved goodbye to her dad as he pulled out of the Redker's College parking lot and then disappeared onto the highway. He'd clearly felt bad about crushing her dreams; otherwise he would never have agreed to drop her off. Back in California, he watched every practice from the bleachers, and he'd give her and her Wheel Friends thumbs-ups as they passed him.

Nat had spent most of the night rehearsing for her audition, but she'd also given a lot of thought to how she'd get there. That morning, she'd told her dad she needed to be at Redker's thirty minutes early to hang out with a few of her new teammates she'd met on the Lightning Wheels Snapchat group. Nat had pinkie-sworn that she'd ask for help transferring into Oakley, her racing chair, which was already stored in the sports facility building, and she'd call her dad if she needed ANYTHING AT ALL. Right now, she needed to slip past Coach Cynthia's office unseen and let go of the guilt she was carrying for lying to her biggest ally.

Nat hid under her helmet and moved toward the tree-lined entrance of the sports building. She rolled past the theater to the bathroom, where she unwrapped her hidden audition outfit from a bag within a bag within a bag and got changed, replacing her nylon legging shorts and tank top with jean shorts, a navy checkered T-shirt, and red flats. She unfolded sheet music from the decoy envelope she'd labeled "Vending Machine Cash" and tucked it in an empty folder. Then she charged out the door, onto the sidewalk, over the crosswalk, and up the ramp to the JCC.

Here. Goes. Literally. Everything.

Inside the building, Nat spotted a cluster of kids around her age plus their parents by some elevator doors. The up button was glowing red. Still, there was a beautiful blond Glinda-type girl—thirteen years old or so—pressing it and pressing it and pressing it until it dinged and parted.

"You coming?" a pale boy in a popped collar polo shirt asked Nat, sticking his frail arm through the closing doors. "We've got room."

"Um, yeah, thanks." Nat zipped in, swiveled around, and stared at the silver doors. In the reflection, she could see everyone wavy and warped, crushed into the corners behind her. Staring. As much as she needed elevators, she hated feeling stuck where dozens of unasked questions about her blew around like balls in a Powerball machine. *Ding!*

The fourth floor was bustling with what must have been a hundred kids. Nat had no idea how many would get cast, but it had to be way less than half. Maybe a quarter. She took a few nervous breaths. If she weren't so sure she was perfect for Nessarose, she would have been hyperventilating. She got swept up in the crowd and ended up near a wall decked out with framed show posters: *Oliver!* and *Fiddler on the Roof* and *Children of Eden* and *Annie* and *Annie Warbucks* (the sequel!). It was the waiting room of her dreams, and she'd gotten there just in time.

"Hi there, everybody!" announced a trendy Black woman with a shaved head and a nose ring. "For those who don't know me, I'm Cora, and I'll be stage-managing this summer's Broadway Bounders' production of *Wicked*!" Nat noticed the desk beside her was littered with headshots and résumés. *Wait . . .* Nat froze in panic. *I don't have a headshot. I don't have a résumé.* "Thanks for being here and offering your talent. It's going to be a *wicked* good time!"

The entire lobby erupted in claps and woos.

"Come see me to sign in," Cora instructed. Then, as if she could read Nat's mind, "Don't be alarmed by the headshots and résumés. If you've got 'em, we'll take 'em. But if you don't, share any stage experience on the application, and we'll take a true-life Instagram." She held up a pink Polaroid camera—the kind that birthed photos on the spot. "Instant headshots."

Nat chuckled with relief alongside . . . just parents.

"And remember," Cora added, slowly scanning the crowd, "the people in the audition room—Calvin and Lulu—they are rooting for you. We are excited to learn about what character you want to play. But, ultimately, we want to see YOU."

Nat suddenly felt her cheeks get hot. She felt like she was in a movie. One of the ones her dad made her watch where all the football players were getting ready to try out, and the underdog was about to—for the first time in his life—blow everyone away.

She wheeled over to the desk, where Cora was already swarmed with kids. In front of Nat was the boy from the elevator. He was talking animatedly to a chubby Indian girl wearing a real bra, not a training one. "My mom says I can't sing in the house at night anymore. Only during office hours."

"What are office hours, again?" the girl asked.

"Nine to five. But I only know that from the musical *9 to 5*."

"Let me guess—your lacrosse-star brothers complained?"

"Yeah. They told my parents, 'Hudson sounds like a gagging goat.' "

"That's 'cause you were practicing 'Something Bad,' a song sung by an *actual* goat."

"Yeah, Rey, but they said it after I was singing normal stuff. Like Rihanna."

"Whatever. It's puberty's fault. They don't get that you're recalibrating your vibrato."

"My pediatrician said I'm delayed, but . . ." He rolled up his sleeve and showed off his armpit. "Hello, twin hairs!"

Nat didn't know Hudson and Rey, but she wanted to be best friends with them. They sounded mature, like mini adults. Also, the way their conversation bounced back and forth reminded her of how she and Chloe talked. Comfortable and funny and in sync. She just had to introduce herself.

"Hey—" Nat went to say, but only got to "Heh" before Hudson very excitedly started talking to Rey about last summer. Nat cleared her throat so they wouldn't think she'd just laughed at their conversation like an old man, but luckily Hudson seemed unfazed, rambling on. "Do you remember when, during 'Supercalifragilisticexpialidocious,' Fig thought Mary Poppins was singing '*Super calloused—*' "

" '*—fragile mystic hexed by halitosis!*' " he and Rey sang together, then broke out in hysterical laughter.

"Wait, what's halitosis again?" Hudson asked.

"BAD BREATH!" Rey practically screamed.

"I'm right *here*," said an olive-skinned boy with purple hair, presumably Fig. "Guys, it was a joke. Of *course* I knew what Poppins was singing. I was practically raised by Walty D."

Nat shoved her hand in her pocket and took out her phone. She stared at it, the apps a blur, as she thought about how all these kids knew each other super well. Chloe would forever be her lifeline, but she still got confused between *Phantom of the Opera* and *Phantom Menace*, the *Star Wars* movie. It would be amazing to share inside jokes with other theater nerds.

"Hey," she tried again as confidently as she could.

"Hey, there," Cora mistakenly replied. She waved Nat forward with one hand, a clipboard in the other, as kids from the side merged center, cutting Nat off. "Hey, guys—*easy*." When they turned around and saw her wheelchair, they parted like the Red Sea.

Nat wheeled to the table, wishing she didn't have to cut the kids in front of her—the very ones she'd been trying to befriend. Hudson's headshot stared up at her. He looked like a Ralph Lauren model in his sweater cardigan and suspenders. Fig's headshot was poking out from underneath it—a classic school picture with a cloudy blue background, his curly hair long and brown, not purple. In Rey's headshot beside it, she was cupping her chin like a cupid, her dress and her bow and the background all white. She looked way different in person, wearing paint-stained khaki shorts, thick-rimmed glasses, and a *Kinky Boots* T-shirt.

"You looking for an application?" Cora asked.

"Uh, yeah," Nat replied.

The Red Sea of theater kids was already closing in around her. Arms swiped pens from a Broadway Bounders mug.

Fingers dropped headshots and résumés. Faces hovered over the sign-in sheet. The closeness was kind of normalizing.

Cora offered Nat an application, and Nat's heart pounded so hard it made her whole body buzz like she was on a train. Actually, the buzzing might have been coming from Hudson, who was now tap-dancing in actual tap shoes to the big *Mary Poppins* number "Step in Time," which was blasting from Rey's phone. He was SENSATIONAL.

"What's your name?" Cora asked.

"Natalie," Nat replied, snapping her head back to the table.

"Natalie, great."

"But you can call me Natty. Or Nat."

"Okay, *Nat*," Cora said crisply, in a way that made it sound like the cool-quirky name of a celebrity's kid. "Why don't you fill out your info away from all the excitement, and we'll take your picture on the way in."

"Cool, sounds good," Nat said. She wheeled to a quiet-ish corner and put Broadway Bounders pen to paper.

Name: Natalie Joy Beacon aka Nat

Address: ....

And . . . already she was stuck. She looked up, half expecting her mom to be there, already writing it in for her. Nat left it blank and moved on.

Hair: Dirty blond, crazy curly. Eyes: Hazel-y. Height: 5'1" / in a wheelchair.

Auditioning for: Nessarose!! Age: 13. Cell Phone Number: 831-555-0116. Email address: JMN@gmail.com.

She crossed out her family's joint email address. She obviously couldn't let her parents get an email before she'd told them what was up.

Next, Theater Experience. Nat tapped her pen against the paper, little dots filling up the corner. Technically, she'd never been in a theater show before. But also, technically, that wasn't the question. Finally, she scribbled:

Matilda's "Revolting Children"—Chorus Soloist—Birch Elementary School

Harry Potter and the Cursed Child—Scorpius Malfoy (read aloud)—Recess Book Club

Annie (one-woman show)—Annie, Molly, Miss Hannigan, etc.—Backyard Productions

Then, for Special Skills: Wheelchair racing (#6 in my age group in CA), singing (mezzo-soprano, but can belt), lyric memorization (I know every word to the Hamilton soundtrack), accents (Californian, Wild West, and British in the style of Oliver!).

And lastly, for Dream Role (just for fun!): Eliza Schuyler Hamilton. Satisfied, Nat dropped her application with Cora, then did a celebratory lap around the lobby to the water fountain. She was one hurdle closer to Nessarose.

The Glinda-type girl was drinking from the fountain, a blond sheet of hair tucked neatly behind her ears. Dangling in her hand was her headshot. It was extremely professional-looking, even more professional than the Hollywood ones Nat had seen on the wall of Gordon's Deli back home. In it, the girl was tugging a jean jacket closed over her chest, and her eyes were so blue, they were sparkling. In funky lettering at the bottom was her name: SAVANNAH ALEXIS.

"Don't judge," said the girl, presumably Savannah Alexis. She dabbed at the water on her lips, then studied her own headshot. "It's really old. I'm getting new ones after the summer."

"Oh, cool," Nat said, trying not to look confused. "How old is it?"

"It's a still shot from my bat mitzvah trailer, so, like, six months."

"Nice." Nat knew what a bat mitzvah was, and she knew what a movie trailer was, but she'd never heard of a bat mitzvah trailer or actors getting new headshots every six months.

"Are you new here?" Savannah asked, twirling her hair around her finger.

"Yeah," Nat replied. "I just moved here from California."

"Omigod, did you, like, see famous people every day?"

"I wish! I didn't live in LA, if that's what you're thinking."

"Oh. Then where *did* you live?"

"The Bay Area."

Savannah shrugged with disinterest, then looked at the elevator like she was waiting for someone to come out of it. "My mom drove home to print a new résumé for me," she explained. "We forgot to take off my earlier experience, like when I played Cruel Carrot in *Veggie Wars.* Plus, my vocal range has expanded to a high C."

"Whoa," Nat said, wondering if she'd ever hit that note when she and Chloe sang opera as a joke. She could go pretty high. "Are you auditioning for Glinda?"

"Um, hold your ponies. How'd you know?"

"Glinda's a soprano."

"I was being sarcastic. Look at me."

"True, true," Nat said, laughing. "I'm Nat, by the way. Short for Natalie."

"Aw, that's such a versatile stage name. Like mine: Savannah Alexis."

Cora's voice suddenly cut through the crowd. "LISTEN UP, AUDITIONEES! WE ARE STARTING! NICOLE SCHNEIDER, MARTI GRUBER, ELI NEWTON—YOU'RE ON DECK!"

Nat's stomach flipped with anticipation.

"Who are *you* auditioning for?" Savannah asked.

"Ha-ha," Nat said, but Savannah didn't crack a smile. She was actually serious. "I'm auditioning for Nessarose—the one in a wheelchair."

Savannah looked down at Nat's legs. "You can get up?"

"No . . . Why?"

"Nessarose is in a wheelchair in act one. But then, in act two, Elphaba gives her the power to walk."

CHAPTER FIVE

Pulled

It took a second for Nat to register what Savannah had just said. Time seemed to slow down, and all she could hear was "walk . . . walk . . . walk" echoing around in her brain. Eventually, Nat snapped out of it, breaking eye contact with Savannah to look down at her wheels. "I've got to— Sorry, I just—" Her face felt like it was inside a preheated oven. "Where's the bathroom?"

Savannah pointed over Nat's head to the other side of the room. Before Nat could thank her, she found herself beelining it to the bathroom. She was doing everything she could to keep the tears in her eyes from streaming down her face. She pushed open the handicap bathroom door, rolled inside, and locked it. Immediately, her eyes became faucets.

I'm so dumb, I'm so dumb. Of course Nessarose gets to walk. Of course the only disabled character I know of in a musical gets magically abled. In theater, anything is possible unless, of course, you're me.

Nat heard a voice through the bathroom door. "Duuuude, are you okay?"

Mortified, Nat swallowed a sob. "Yeah, uh, just warming up." She pressed the hand dryer to diffuse the sound of her not warming up and gathered wads of toilet paper to dry her face.

She heard another knock and burst into the first chorus warm-up that popped into her head. "*Chester cheetah chewed a chunk of cheap cheddar cheese!*" She sang it on repeat, going up a semitone each time. Her voice got beltier as a ball of rage grew in her belly.

The hand dryer stopped, and Nat heard pounding. Out of excuses, she swung open the convulsing door. It was the girl in the *Kinky Boots* T-shirt, Rey. She was wincing, hopping up and down with her legs crossed. "Sorry. Gotta pee. Someone threw up in the other bathroom. Auditions are crazy. Gracias." And then, before Nat knew it, Rey was inside the bathroom and she was not.

It was time to leave. Nat pushed toward the elevator at racing speed, when she felt Peaches hit a bump. "Gah!" In a panic, she glanced down at a spotless silver Nike high-top. "Sorry! Are you okay?! I'm so sorry!"

"It's cool," a boy said, kneeling to smooth out a dent in his left sneaker. He was cute. Maybe even the cutest boy Nat had ever seen—in life, on TV, anywhere. Perfect dark skin, giant brown eyes, and dreads tied back in a baby-blue bandanna. "My mom bought these kicks in a size up so I'd grow into them, so you missed my toe."

"Oh, good. That's good."

He stood and then looked at her, awaking butterflies in her belly. "Was that you singing in the bathroom?"

"Oh, I—" Nat needed to lie: She only sang sophisticated warm-ups, not ones about wildcats and cheese. But her head was nodding in betrayal.

"Whoa," he said, his giant eyes growing gigantic. "Your voice is crazy good."

"Ha, thanks." Nat had gotten compliments on her voice before. Her chorus teacher once told her she had "cords made for choir," and Chloe had once compared her sound to Ariana Grande's. It had felt good. But hearing it now, from Cute Boy, it made her feel like she was levitating. Nat smiled and darted her eyes to the floor. His high-tops, her flats—they were unmoving in a sea of shuffling sneakers and character shoes. *Say something else, Nat. Don't end this.* "Oh, and you too."

"You've heard me sing?" the boy asked.

Nope. "I just meant I bet you have a nice voice, too."

The boy smiled, flashing baby-blue braces. "I really like to sing. I asked my mom for lessons, but you're not supposed to train until you're more mature. Your vocal cords are more mature, I mean."

"Oh, ha. That makes sense." Thirty seconds passed. Or maybe it was two.

"I'm Malik, by the way," he said, sticking his hand out.

Nat was suddenly feeling her heart in her palms, pulsing wildly. She nervously went to shake back, and Malik flattened her hand with a slap that slid into a snap.

"I'm Nat," she told him.

"Nat. Cool, cool."

"Have you done the show here before?" she asked, hoping he'd say no and they'd have that to bond over.

"Yeah," he said. "Every summer for the last three years."

"Wow. That's a lot of years."

Nat watched him wave to a white girl across the room who had frizzy brown hair popping out from underneath a *Hadestown* baseball cap. She bent her knees and started snapping toward them, like she was a Jet from *West Side Story*. When she got to Malik, he gave her a high five. Nat caught sight of a pin fastened to her floral romper that read CAN'T. IT'S TECH WEEK.

"I'm Jaclyn, waz up?"

"Nat, nothin' much."

And then Jaclyn snapped toward Fig, surprising him by jumping onto his back like a koala. He collapsed to the floor.

"Anyway," Malik said, "I love it here. You'll love it, too."

"Yeah, maybe."

"Why 'maybe'?"

The elevator dinged, and Nat was suddenly reminded that she had been on her way out. It was time to go back to the Lightning Wheels and tell Coach Cynthia she was so sorry that she was late, she'd gotten kidnapped or something. "This probably isn't the best summer for me to audition," she admitted.

"What do you mean? You don't like *Wicked*?"

"I love *Wicked*," Nat explained. "But I'm not sure *Wicked* loves me."

Malik looked at her funny. "You'll get in. With your voice, they'd have to be high on stage paint not to take you."

"NATALIE BEACON, YOU'RE ON DECK!" Cora shouted.

Nat's heart nearly leaped out of her chest. She twisted her torso toward the check-in table with her fingernails digging into her wheels. She'd have to make a break for it.

"That's you, right?" Malik asked.

Nat twisted back to him. "Yeah, it's just—" *Tell him you're leaving.* "I guess I should—" *Tell him you don't have the guts.* "That's me, yeah."

"Break a leg!" Malik said, and then, clearly mortified, "Er, dang. That was dumb."

"It's fine," she said, because it totally was. "Seriously."

"You're gonna destroy."

Nat chuckled a nervous thanks, her brain a mess of thoughts. *Am I doing this? I'm not doing this, am I? No, no way.* She began to wheel herself toward Cora while also looking for a spot to cut away to the elevator. She went around Hudson, the tap dancer, who was stretching on the floor, pointing and flexing; by Fig and Jaclyn, who were poofing out each other's curls with their fingers while trilling their own lips; and past Savannah and her mom poring over her newly printed résumé. There was no good spot to get away, and even if there were, what if Malik was watching? What would he think if she ditched him? Nat didn't have a choice. She'd have to audition. She'd miss her first racing practice, mess up her chance at being on the team, disappoint her dad, freak out her mom, and never be trusted again.

She arrived breathless. She must have forgotten to breathe.

"Hi, Nat. Go right there against the wall for me, please." Cora pointed between the framed show posters of *Footloose* and *All Shook Up*. Nat wheeled herself into place, smoothed out the frizzies in her hair, and forced a smile. The camera flashed and snapped, and an old-school square photo shot out. Cora waved it toward her like a fan, then stapled it to Nat's application. The outline of Nat's face started to appear like a ghost. "All right, take this into the room with you, and make sure your sheet music is handy."

Nat dropped the application on her lap. She wished her makeshift headshot looked professional like Savannah Alexis's perfect one. She didn't have much time to harp on it, though—Cora swung the door open, and Nat was already wheeling herself inside.

The space reminded her of her middle school's choir classroom: big and open with a piano and a semicircle of bleachers. The door closed behind her, and she felt her hands start to shake. She gave the wavering application to a white man with a *Newsies* cap and a name tag that read CALVIN, DIRECTOR. She then did five big wheels away. She'd seen enough actor documentaries to know she shouldn't sing too close to the casting table but not too far from it, either.

"What are you singing today, Nat?" Calvin asked her, examining her application.

" 'Rainbow.' I mean 'Over the Rainbow,' and I chose the song because, well, you know. *The Wizard of Oz*. Ha." *Get. It. Together.* "Oh! And I have the sheet music."

The accompanist—whose name tag read LULU, MUSIC DIRECTOR—smirked. "I think I've got that one memorized." She shook her choppy brown hair, placed her fingers on the piano keys, and without any warning, started to play the introduction.

Also without warning, Nat started to have an out-of-body experience. She felt like she was floating beside Calvin at the casting table, watching herself audition. The air was heavy, and the piano was dull, and time was slooooooow. She heard Malik's voice say, "You're crazy good," and, suddenly, it clicked: It didn't matter that she couldn't play Nessarose. She had a killer voice. That's what had driven her to skip racing and give this her all. She was going to do well, going to do amazing, going to knock it out of the ballpark, out of New Jersey, all the way to California and beyond! *Here. We. Go!*

She'd missed her cue. Nat was back in her body, and her heart was slamming. Lulu eyed her with polite pity, then repeated the introduction. She had her chin cocked, ready to nod.

One more chance. Nat took a deep breath, but the oxygen seemed to stop at her shoulders. Her mouth felt like cardboard.

Lulu nodded. It was actually so enthusiastic, it was more like a head bang. The chord rang out, and Nat started to sing.

Her shoulders relaxed. Her hands stopped trembling. She loosened her grip on her chair, then let go of it entirely. Her eyes were open, but she wasn't seeing Lulu or Calvin, or even the chorus-like room at all. She was outside by Auntie Em and Uncle Henry's barn—the sepia movie set of the original *Wizard of Oz.* Her thoughts were swirling, but not as Nat. As Dorothy. She imagined Warbucks as Toto, panting by her side. She thought about finding them a place where there wasn't any trouble. A place that was far, far away. Beyond New Jersey, beyond the Bay Area, even. A place where she could slip on ruby-red slippers and make new best friends along the way.

Nat blinked, and she was no longer in Kansas. She'd sung the whole song. Or at least a cut of it. She had no idea.

"Thanks so much," said Calvin. "Very nice rendition."

"Agreed," said Lulu. "Wonderful work."

Wonderful work, work, work. It seemed to echo.

"Thanks, I'm glad it was— I'm glad you both thought so," Nat replied. She could feel her blood pumping as if she'd just wheeled up a mountain. How was she so excited and totally exhausted at the same time?! Had she nailed it? Had she messed up? Had she cracked? Had she wowed them? Had she? Had she? Had she? Aaaaaaaaaah!

"Before you go," Calvin said, stopping Nat in her tracks before she even realized she'd begun wheeling herself toward the door, "the casting email goes out tomorrow at four PM. Want to write an email address down so we can contact you?"

"Oh. Yeah," Nat said, then jotted down the only other email address she could think of: Doctb@gmail.com.

"You want to be a doctor?" asked Calvin.

No. I hate doctors. They're the worst. "Only if the whole acting thing doesn't work out."

He and Lulu shared a grin. Then they stared at her, cueing her to leave.

Nat wheeled herself out, a text to Chloe already forming in her head: "A cast list for *Wicked* is crashing your inbox in 29 hours. Looooong story—talk tn?"

OZ BOUNDERZ

DearEvanHudson: It's 3:42, people! 18 min till casting! SOMEONE DISTRACT ME!!!

TheReyWhereItHappens: 🐱 👟 😥

DearEvanHudson: THAT'S NOT DISTRACTING U USE THOSE EMOJIS EVERY DAY

JACLYNandHYDE: There's a rumor i made up that we didn't get the rights to Wicked

JACLYNandHYDE: so we are putting on Follies instead

JACLYNandHYDE: and we'll all have to wear old-age makeup and im dead with joy

TheSoundOfMalik: u've always had the soul of a 78 yr old

JACLYNandHYDE: thank you sincerely young man

TheReyWhereItHappens: lolz ur last name is Young

TheSoundOfMalik: haha yeah. yoooo, i'm adding Savannah

PurpleHairyPoppins: I got the email. I'm playing the Wizard. Huzzah!

DearEvanHudson: WHAT?! YOU GOT THE EMAIL?!?!?????

TheReyWhereItHappens: Hud, chill, he's joking

PurpleHairyPoppins: My baaaad. I meant I'm playing Elphaba.

LegallySavannah: ummm, who added me 2 this group chat?!

TheSoundOfMalik: me

LegallySavannah: oh, haha, LOLZ, coooooool

PurpleHairyPoppins: Actually, Glinda.

LegallySavannah: yea?

PurpleHairyPoppins: I was joking that I got cast as Glinda.

LegallySavannah: hahahahaha!

PurpleHairyPoppins: I wasn't calling you Glinda.

LegallySavannah: Fig, ur sooooo dumb.

LegallySavannah: Malik, what r u doing tmrw?

DearEvanHudson: Get. A. Room.

TheReyWhereItHappens: 🔥

JACLYNandHYDE: 🎟

TheSoundOfMalik: Jac, u still have access to the numbers of the kids who auditioned?

JACLYNandHYDE: yeh ima stalker.

JACLYNandHYDE: jk. Malik and i helped cora enter everyone's info into Google Sheets—cora shared w/ me so we could do it on my phone

PurpleHairyPoppins: y?

JACLYNandHYDE: Our parents were late picking us up and we were booooored

TheSoundOfMalik: can u text me the new girl nat's # pls? im gonna invite her 2 chat

CHAPTER SIX

I Hope I Get It

Nat sat on her bed, binge-eating goldfish. She glanced at her phone. 3:49 PM. She checked that the ringer was on. It was. She composed *one more* text to Chloe. "Chlo! U get my messages?? Call me when u get the email from B'way Bounders! Heart emoji. Drama Masks emoji. Starry-eyed emoji. Nervous Cat emoji." *Whoosh!*

Just as Nat was starting to fall into another worry spiral—Why hadn't Chloe called her back? Had she gotten the email? Was it bad news?—Idina Menzel's power belt erupted from her phone. "*It's time to try, defy—*"

"CHLOE!" Nat burst out, picking up.

"Hey, Nat!" Chloe whispered.

"Did the email come? Did I get in?!"

"What? Oh. No. I dunno."

Nat pulled her phone from her ear to check the time again. 3:50 PM. How had only one minute passed? She fumbled to put the conversation on speaker.

". . . one free slot, and I'm literally flying!!!"

"Cool!" Nat said. "So, you're home now or . . . ?"

"Home? No. I'm in a Golden Gate Park bathroom. It smells awesome in here."

"Ha. So, when will you be home?"

"Well, the program goes till four o' clock."

Nat quickly did the math. It was almost four o' clock in New Jersey. That meant, with the three-hour time difference, it was almost one o' clock in California. Whatever program Chloe was talking about, she wouldn't be home till 7:30 New Jersey time. Nat would have to wait three and a half hours. *Unless* . . . "Wait! Do you get email on your phone?"

"Nope."

"But *can* you get emails?"

"Maybe? I'd have to check if it's set up."

"Cool!" Nat held her breath, literally, while she waited for Chloe to check. But then, after three and a half Mississippis, Chloe began talking about something called a carabiner, and Nat exhaled, ready to lose her mind. "Are you checking your phone for email?!"

"I'm peeing. Can you hear it?"

"No." Suddenly, a flushing sound blared. It was so loud Nat might as well have been inside a toilet. "You got my messages, right? About Wicked?"

"Yeah. You love musicals. That's awesome, Natty! Congrats!"

"Ha, don't congratulate me yet! It depends on the email. You'll call me? Like as soon as you get it?"

"Yeah, of course. I got you. You're still gonna race, though, right?"

Nat swallowed a groan. "It depends on the email." On the word "email," a near-blinding light bulb switched on in her brain. "Wait, what's your password?!"

"Ummm . . . I think it's my parents' anniversary with a twist. It's saved on my computer, but I don't have it memorized." Nat's heart dipped as another surround-sound flush blared through the phone. "Is your dad freaking out?" Chloe asked. "I feel like he'd act so weird if you quit racing."

From across the room, Nat's laptop lit up and made a *baloop* sound. "Did you just chat me?"

"Why would I chat you? We're talking on the phone."

"Weird, hold on." Nat shoved her phone in her pocket. She pulled her legs to the side of the bed, lined Peaches up at a diagonal, and transferred in. She wheeled over to her laptop so fast she practically crashed into her desk. Waiting for her was an invitation to a group chat called *Oz Bounderz.*

Nat's hand hovered over the keyboard until her fingertip started pulsing. She pressed down, accepting. *Swhoop, swhoop, swhoop, swhoop, swhoop, swhoop, swhoop.* A chat flooded her screen.

LegallySavannah: You'll B Fiyero I know it.

PurpleHairyPoppins: thanx, boo

JACLYNandHYDE: lolz Fig

DearEvanHudson: who r u talking about, Savannah?

TheReyWhereItHappens: 🤣

LegallySavannah: Malik. Fiyero's character is inspired by the scarecrow in The Wizard of Oz but in Wicked he's the romantic lead.

TheSoundOfMalik: Nat u here?

Yes, she was. Hyperventilating. *This is real. Historical. You've been invited to your first-ever group chat. Don't mess it up*. Nat shook out her hands and plopped them down on the keyboard, accidentally typing, "sjkdfjdldsjkfjd." Delete! Her heart was in her fingers—*pulse, pulse, pulse*. She tried again.

NatThrowinAwayMyShot: Yeah hi! How'd u get my username?

TheSoundOfMalik: It's hooked up to your #

PurpleHairyPoppins: Malik + Jac = Smooth stalkin'.

JACLYNandHYDE: that's the name of my future podcast

TheReyWhereItHappens: I'm Reyna. U can call me Rey.

TheReyWhereItHappens: I'm the one who kicked you out of the bathroom cuz my bladder was gonna explode. I ♥ your username.

NatThrowinAwayMyShot: Hi! Hamilton! Yes!

TheReyWhereItHappens: Ham gals unite!

NatThrowinAwayMyShot: Hahahaha!

Nat noticed she was laughing. OUT LOUD. Rey's username was a play on the *Hamilton* song "The Room Where It Happens." Nat's username was a play on the *Hamilton* lyrics "*Not throwing away my shot*." They were just two fangirls chatting online—NO BIG DEAL.

TheSoundOfMalik: Hey yo! everyone say who u are so Nat knows.

TheReyWhereItHappens: Rey, but I just told u that

DearEvanHudson: Hudson, hey!

JACLYNandHYDE: I'm Jaclyn or Jac or whatevs. We met yesterday, waz uuuuup

PurpleHairyPoppins: Eli Newton's the name, but everyone calls me Fig.

LegallySavannah: It's me! Savannah Alexis. We talked at the water fountain.

Nat wasn't very religious, but her fingers were suddenly clasped together, and she was praying in her head, *Please, God, let me get cast in this musical. Let me become best friends with these people.* She went to compliment everyone on their usernames when another stream of *swhoops* flooded the screen.

DearEvanHudson: They emailed it.

LegallySavannah: OMG

PurpleHairyPoppins: Wizzy Wizzzzzz, Wazzup

TheReyWhereItHappens: First. Legit. Role!
JACLYNandHYDE: What the WITCH!!!!!!!!!!!!!
TheSoundOfMalik: So happy for all a ya!
TheReyWhereItHappens: 🍍🌞⚡
DearEvanHudson: The character Boq dances a lot, right? What's his deal again?
TheReyWhereItHappens: We LOVE each other, Hud.
LegallySavannah: Actually, YOU love HIM. HE loves ME. And I love FIYERO. 😝

Nat jerked her phone from her pocket. She had a missed call from Chloe. She'd totally forgotten about her. Chloe had probably been worried, having listened to Nat crash into her desk, power-type, and laugh psychotically to herself.

Nat pressed the green phone icon. It began ringing as the Oz Bounderz rapidly exchanged more emojis: Rainbow. Comet. Chili Pepper. Bowling Ball. Chopsticks. Pushpin.

"It's Chlo, as you know. Leave a message, and I'll call you back!" *Beeeeeeeep.*

"Hey, Chlo! It's me. Sorry about that. I, um . . ."

Lobster. Pencil. Red Heart. Blue Heart.

"The casting email got sent out, and I'm . . ."

Spoon. Another Spoon. Another, another Spoon.

"Gah! I can't right now. Call me back!!!"

Nat hung up and stared at the new emojis pouring in on her laptop. Maybe the Recycling Symbol meant an old set piece could be recycled. Maybe the Loudspeaker was a comment on the mic system. Maybe the Mailbox meant the casting email was also getting snail-mailed. Or maybe none of it meant anything at all.

Her heart slamming, Nat couldn't wait any longer. "I didn't get the email," she typed. "Can someone paste it into the chat?"

Between a tirade of Lettuces, Malik sent a thumbs-up.

"Thank u!!!" Nat wrote back, then frantically waited with a real-life thumbs-up in her mouth. More emoji filled the chat. "Malik, did u send yet?!" she typed, but deleted. "Malik, did u send yet?!" she actually sent.

A fresh message from Malik surfaced, the cast list! Nat tried to focus her suddenly blurry vision and read fast, frantically scouring the list for her name. *Where's the "N"? Where's the "a"? Where's the "t"? What does that spell? Nat! Where are they together?! I DON'T KNOW!*

Broadway Bounders Cast List
WICKED

Elphaba—Jaclyn Arazi

Glinda—Savannah Alexis

Fiyero—Malik Young

Boq—Hudson Tucker-Stone

Wizard of Oz—Eli "Fig" Newton

Nessarose—Reyna Joshi

Doctor Dillamond—Kyle Bindler

Madame Morrible—Gia Giordano

Witch's Father—Steven Chung

Witch's Mother—Jayden Prior

Midwife—Caitlin Clark

Chistery—Erica Wolf

Monkeys, Students, Denizens of the Emerald City, Palace Guards, and other Citizens of Oz—Sabine Alsadder, Natalie Beacon, Avi Davidson, Amy Lu Gang, Marti Gruber, Molly Massey-Todd, Aiden Pax, Kyra Rodriguez, Nicole Schneider, Leeza Smart, Petey Smith, Madden Weinberger—

Nat stopped reading when she reached her name. She blinked. Then a super-happy tear slid out from the corner of her eyeball, splashing onto the H key. She didn't care. What did she need the H key for, anyway?! What did she even need her laptop for?! She'd be hanging out with the Broadway Bounders in person every day for four weeks, playing a monkey or a student or a denizen (whatever that was) or a palace guard or a citizen of Oz or maybe ALL OF THE ABOVE!

Nat had to tell them. "*MOM! DAD!*"

She heard the clacking of heels and the pounding of sneakers. There were two fast knocks on her bathroom door, and then it just swung open. Her mom lurched inside the room and stopped short. Her dad slammed into her.

Nat could feel her smiling mouth get scared into a line. She'd hollered before she'd even known what she was going to say. "I auditioned for *Wicked*," she blurted out.

And then, not mad but like he'd misheard, her dad asked, "You what?"

"I auditioned for *Wicked*."

Her parents let that sink in. Her dad went as frozen as an ice sculpture, and her mom's face scrunched so hard with confusion that her two eyebrows looked like they were one.

"Do you *CARE* to *EXPLAIN*?" her mom asked, loud and shrill.

Nat didn't. She wished she'd kept it all a secret just a bit longer. At least long enough to celebrate with a song, call Chloe with the news, and pick out her first rehearsal outfit.

"*Well?*" her mom pressed, thrusting out two rigid hands.

Nat took a shallow breath. "I was at racing practice, and I just— I left. I went to the JCC and met all these really cool people and sang 'Over the Rainbow' and I just found out—I got in." She swallowed dry, hard air. "I'm so sorry I lied. I'm so sorry."

Nat prayed that her parents would miraculously accept her apology and congratulate her with a giant hug! But then, a lot, like *a lot* of seconds passed, and the only sounds that came out of them were constipated grunts from her dad and flabbergasted *Hmms* from her mom.

Her dad finally unfroze just enough to say, "I'm honestly afraid to ask how you logistically made this happen."

And then, unafraid to ask, her mom went, "What do you mean you 'left' practice? How did you get to the JCC?"

Nat stared into her lap, trying to ignore the blood pulsing in her ears. "It's across the street, so, yeah."

"Do you know how many things could have gone wrong in just you getting there?!" her mom carried on. "I don't even want to run the math on that."

"Nothing went wrong," Nat tried to assure her. "I got there safely, and everyone was really nice."

"Who? The staff?" her dad asked. "Do they understand what you need? Exactly what did you tell them?"

Nat cocked her chin in disbelief. "I didn't tell them anything, because I didn't need to," she asserted. "I auditioned like everyone else. And I got in! All on my own!"

Her dad spoke sharply. "Look, Nat. You *lied to us* and did the thing we told you that you couldn't do. You *ditched racing* and, sidebar—I can't believe Cynthia never bothered to check in!" He crossed his arms. "I just— I'm worried for you that *this show* won't be all you want it to be."

"You're not thinking this through, Nat," her mom agreed.

"YES, I AM!" Nat yelled. Her parents were smothering her so hard they'd basically FORCED her to lie. And how were they still so worried?! Were they not registering the fact that she'd auditioned and gotten into the show ALL BY HERSELF? If that didn't make them believe in her, then what would?!

In the thick silence, Nat's mom's face slowly relaxed. "Natty, this is what you want?" she asked softly. "You're one hundred percent sure?"

Nat nodded enthusiastically. "More percent," she answered, and then looked at her dad in the hope he was softening, too. His eyes were shut, and he was swaying gently in thought. "Dad?"

He stopped moving, opened his eyes, and said begrudgingly, "You know, Nat, I don't even know why we're having this conversation when you've clearly already made up your mind."

Nat tried not to let that punch derail her. There was too much at stake. "So, that's a yes?"

Her parents looked at each other, figured something out telepathically, and then looked back at her. Tired, her dad said, "Prove to us we're not out of our minds for letting you do this."

Nat gasped and then smiled so big it hurt. "Okay! Yes! I will!"

CHAPTER SEVEN

The History of Wrong Guys

"HELLO, WITCHES AND WIZARDS AND DENIZENS OF OZ! As most of you know, I'm Calvin Mackintosh, the director of Broadway Bounders." Calvin tapped a wireless mic and stepped to the front of the stage. "WELCOME TO THE FIRST REHEARSAL FOR *WICKED*!"

The cast went wild. Even though Nat had counted fewer than thirty people in an auditorium that could easily fit two hundred, their excitement charged the whole space. The theater was on the same floor as the room she'd auditioned in, and even though this was only her second time in the building, the JCC was already starting to feel like a place where she belonged. It didn't hurt that she'd arrived at the same time as Malik, who'd sweetly waved for her to follow him to the third row, where he'd plopped down beside her in the aisle seat.

Calvin silenced the applause by closing his fingers into a fist and went on. "I'm lucky to be joined by the dynamic duo: Lulu and Coraaaaaaa!" He pointed to Lulu at the piano, and she ran her fingers up the keys. Then he pointed to Cora in the front row, and she whipped a flashlight out from her tool belt and shined it around the audience. More claps. More woos.

Cora spoke next. "So, as detailed in the email, we'll be holding rehearsals every weekday from ten AM to five PM, with a half-hour break for lunch. This week, we'll be learning music, blocking, and choreography."

A boy's hand shot up from the first row. "What's blocking?"

Nat bit her lip, waiting for some know-it-all chuckles from the program veterans, but no one made a peep. "Good question, Petey," Calvin answered. He looked at Hudson, sitting front-row center beside Rey. "Hey, dance captain, care to take this one?"

"Totes!" Hudson exclaimed, jumping up from his seat with the perfect verticalness of a pogo stick. "Blocking is the choreography of acting," he said, which sounded philosophical and confusing.

Now Rey stood up. "I'll break it down. Blocking is when Calvin tells us, 'Say your line and then go stage left. No, the *other* stage left.' "

There was instant, all-knowing laughter.

Calvin raised an eyebrow. "Thank you, Hudson and Rey, for tag-teaming that explanation," he teased. "I hope this summer we can all graduate masters of stage directions."

More chuckles. Nat was going to have to look up and memorize "stage directions" STAT.

"So, we are all aware this is not a *school* production. That being said, I'm assigning some—*dun dun dun*—reading!" Calvin reached into a messenger bag at his feet and whipped out a book. The cover looked identical to the *Wicked* show poster—an artsy graphic of Glinda whispering into Elphaba's ear. "*Wicked* is a musical based on this novel, *Wicked: The Life and Times of the Wicked Witch of the West.* I want you to get to know your characters. The ensemble especially: Allow the supporting characters in the book to inspire who you become onstage. Remember, there are no small parts, only small actors."

While the cast CLAPPED IT UP FOR SUMMER READING, Nat straightened her posture. She wasn't a small actor. She was a great big one who would study that book from cover to cover. Maybe she'd discover a character named Belinda, who was Glinda's jealous best friend and a baker who misused her magic by selling cursed cakes. Or maybe she'd discover a character named Selphaba, who was Elphaba's soul sister and a social justice warrior who inspired change through slam poetry!

Suddenly, Nat felt a nudge on her shoulder. "I read it already," Malik whispered, holding out his own copy of the book. "Want it?"

"Are you sure?" Nat whispered back, reluctantly taking it. She did a quick flip-through, noticing he'd penciled a lot of notes in the margins. "You don't want it for the rehearsal process?"

Malik shrugged. "We can share."

Share? Nat thought giddily. *Like, we both write notes in the margins that are to ourselves but really to each other?*

Before she could even thank Malik, Calvin declared, "LET'S WARM UP!" and kids from the first two rows started stampeding toward the stage.

"Wanna, um—?" Malik asked politely.

Unclog the row? Sorry, yeah. Nat dropped her backpack to the floor and rolled down the aisle toward the stairs leading up to the stage. Yup, THE STAIRS. Only a few feet from them, she veered off to the side, scouring for a ramp. The stampede was rapidly thinning as two kids at a time charged up the stairs. Nat tried to meet eyes with Calvin, but a mass of kids was closing in on him. She spotted Cora at the piano, but she and Lulu were occupied, too, poring over a thick binder with color-coded tabs.

"Nat Throwin' Away My Shot!"

Nat looked up to the stage at Rey. "Hey!" she said, throwing her pointer finger in the air like the *Hamilton* logo. "How do—?"

Rey was already shoving her way down the stairs. "Follow me," she said, leading Nat to a wooden door that blended perfectly into the wall. She pushed it open with a swing of her hip. "Ow. Ha."

"You okay?"

"Ask me tomorrow."

Nat followed Rey to the lip of a long metal ramp that led backstage. Special entrances were usually a hassle, but something about Rey's chillness made Nat feel like less of a burden. In fact, Rey made Nat feel so unburdensome, she didn't even have to gather her courage to ask, "Hey, do you mind giving me a pull?"

Rey outstretched her hand, and Nat grabbed it, zipping up the ramp way faster than she'd expected. "Whoa!" Nat exclaimed. "How are you so strong?!"

Rey kissed her bicep. "Field hockey. Arm muscles are a thing."

Nat laughed. "Just a heads-up, I'll probably ask you to do this for me again. Like, tomorrow. And the next day."

"Anytime. To be honest, you're super light. Still, I'm gonna add 'high-intensity, low-duration arms' to my daily workout log. You'll vouch for me?"

"Sure, yeah. Anything."

"My coach will be thrilled."

Nat and Rey moved to the stage, where the cast was circled up and buzzing with chatter. Nat self-consciously tugged her pink spandex shorts closer to her knees and untangled the self-made fringes on her Earth Day T-shirt.

"LISTEN UP!" Calvin shouted through his hands, which were cupped around his mouth like a megaphone.

"I'm going to be leading you through a bunch of different warm-ups each rehearsal to get your voices and bodies connected and ready." He dropped his hands, and somehow his volume went up. "FOLLOW MY LEAD!"

Malik appeared beside Nat, tightening a bandanna he had definitely not been sporting earlier. It was hot pink, like her shorts. "Hey," he said, tucking a loose dread behind his ear.

"Hey," Nat replied, doing the same with one of her ringlets.

He leaned in, like he was about to tell her a secret. "Warning: Some of these warm-ups are weird, but they're actually really fun if you give 'em a shot. If you get lost, say a code word or whatever, and I'll help."

"A code word?" Nat asked.

Malik looked across the circle at Fig's retro *Sesame Street* shirt. "Yeah. Like 'Elmo.' "

"I'm pretty sure if I randomly say 'Elmo,' someone is going to think *I'm* the weird one."

"Okay then, um"—he turned around to find inspiration—" 'mop.' "

"Oh yeah, that's way more normal."

"Want to just say 'Normal'?"

Nat laughed so hard, so suddenly, some spit got stuck in her throat. Luckily, the old Sia hit "Chandelier" came bursting through the speakers, so Malik didn't notice.

"All right, everyone," Calvin began over the music. "Follow me to the best of your ability. Feel the music, and let your body take you where it needs to go."

Nat wasn't judging the weirdness at all, but she'd be lying if she said she didn't notice it. Calvin began by lifting his arms up over his head, then dropping to a squat and crooning, "*One thing you might not know about me*," then pointing at everyone to repeat him. They did. He shared, "My name is Calvin, and this is my fifth summer directing and choreographing a Broadway Bounders show!" He cued everyone to sing again, "*One thing you might not know about me*," while sweeping his arms around his calves. With every movement came a dramatic breath. He looked like a ballerina giving birth standing up. Still, everyone was GOING FOR IT, so Nat went for it, too. She did all the dance stretches, except the leg ones. But that was okay—everyone seemed to be modifying the moves. Some kids were doing less-exaggerated versions. Some kids—er, just Hudson and Fig—were doing MORE-exaggerated versions, which made them look like they were swimming in maple syrup. Nat used the leg-stretch time to roll out her neck. She cut a glance at Malik, who was concentrating so hard on following Calvin's every step, his tongue was flipped up over his top lip. He broke his concentration to smile at Nat, totally unbashful, and she smiled back. *Bring on all the weird.*

Switching modes, Calvin began snapping.

Fig, who'd probably done this exercise before, stumbled into the middle of the circle as if someone had pushed him. "My name is Fig, and I once ate alligator meat and then met the alligator in my dream."

"*One thing you might not know about me.*" The singing happened between every share.

"My name is Jaclyn, and I get really stressed out when I'm running late."

"My name is Avi, and my cat is on Prozac, which is making him so much friendlier!"

"My name is Marti, and harmonies are really hard for me."

"My name is Nicole, and I was once in a Kars4Kids commercial."

Nat soaked it all in, trying to memorize everyone's names and quirks. She realized she should share. She'd have to, probably.

"My name is Molly, and everyone in my family has red hair, including my pointer pup!"

"My name is Sabine, and I run cross-country in the fall."

"My name is Leeza, and folktronica music feeds my soul."

"My name is Savannah, duh, and Glinda is a part I was born to play."

Nat snapped the spandex on her shorts. *What should I say?* Something funny? Something cute-sad? Something relatable?

"My name is Erica, and I babysit weekends if y'all could get the word out."

"My name is Steven, and I freelance as a school campaign manager."

"Hudson, here. I broke three toes when I was four and still refused to stop tap-dancing."

"My name is Aiden, and I'm a bot."

Thirteen kids had gone. Nat would have to share soon. Nineteen kids. Like, really soon.

"I'm Rey, and when the cast of *SpongeBob* signed my *Playbill*, I slept with it."

"I'm Malik, and dancing makes me a better basketball player during the school year."

Twenty-one kids. The game turned to white noise. Twenty-three kids. The white noise became no noise.

"Did everyone go?" Calvin asked. "I want everyone to share. Last chance!"

Dozens of eyes drifted toward her. Nat ran her fingers through the fringes of her T-shirt so that they fully covered her midriff, then wheeled into the center of the circle. "My name is Nat, and um . . ."

Her mind sped up like a windshield in the rain. Should she share the time she and Chloe wrote a love letter to Tropicana and got sent a package of orange magnets? No, too much of an inside joke. *Wipe.* Should she share that her support dog, Warbucks, flunked training? No, someone might ask why she has a support dog. *Wipe.* Should she share her obsession with *Hamilton*? No, that's also Rey's thing. *Wipe.*

"Um, let's see . . . I don't . . ."

The silence was deafening. Until there was a clap. Then another. Then another. A series of slow solo claps became a series of faster group claps. And then the cast began cheering over one another. FOR HER.

"Yeah, Nat, you got this!" went Hudson.

"Go, girl, go!" went Rey.

"Woo-woo-woo!" went Fig.

"Do YOU!" went Malik.

Nat could feel her face turn *Annie*-hair red. *Annie!* That was it! "Okay, my name is Nat!" she called over them, leaking nervous giggles. "And even though I've been obsessed with musical theater ever since I saw *Annie*, this is the first time I've ever been in a show."

The clapping exploded into a clap storm. No joke. Nat could hardly control the bigness of her smile. She'd made the right choice auditioning, the best choice. She'd believed in herself and stumbled into the coolest, most supportive group of theater nerds she never knew existed.

She felt on top of the world.

She stayed there, on top of the world, as Cora distributed the score and Lulu broke everyone into voice parts:

soprano, alto, tenor, and bass. She stayed there, on top of the world, as she sang out by the piano on the opening number "No One Mourns the Wicked" and recorded her soprano part on her phone. She stayed there, on top of the world, as she volunteered for and got offered the first solo line of the entire show, "Look! It's Glinda!" She stayed there, on top of the world, as she ate her turkey sandwich with the kids from the Oz Bounderz chat group. At 4:00 PM, she was still there, on top of the world, as Calvin started to transition the ensemble plus Fiyero, Glinda, and dance captain, Hudson, back to the stage to learn the first bit of choreography for "Dancing Through Life" while the rest of the leads ran their lines in the room where the auditions had been held.

Nat was pushing toward the ramp, when Calvin waved her to a corner. "So, Nat—quick chat?" he asked. She followed him, bubbling with curiosity. Maybe he'd compliment her on her solo, or give her another solo, or ask her who she wanted to be paired with for the dancing. Malik. She'd say Malik.

"On behalf of the entire creative team and cast, we are so glad you're joining us this summer. Everyone's excited to work with you."

"So excited to work with you and everyone, too," she told him, realizing that Malik was Fiyero, so he and Savannah would most definitely be paired together.

"You, uh, have access to the novel?"

"The *Wicked* book? Yeah, I'm going to start reading tonight."

"That's great," Calvin said, briefly catching eyes with Cora. He gave her a *Go-ahead* nod, and she started modeling an eight-count with Hudson. It looked complicated.

Nat gripped her wheels, ready to roll. "Should I . . . ?"

"I've got good news for you."

So, it *was* a solo! Or maybe, MAYBE, an upgrade to an *actual part*! In her head, Nat began singing the chorus's opening lyric of the show, "*GOOD NEWS!*"

"I want to let you know that you can head home for the day."

Wait, what?! In her head, Nat sang the second lyric of the show, "*SHE'S DEAD!*"

Calvin explained. "We're teaching the ensemble the choreography for one of the most intense numbers of the show. We think it's best for you to sing the song, not worry about all the movement."

Not worry about the movement?! She followed his gaze to the stage, where the ensemble was now paired off, mostly boy-girl, in two perfectly windowed lines. Front and center were Malik and Savannah. She had her arms around his shoulders. His arms were around her waist. He lifted her, and she swung her legs up past his left side, then his right. They looked great together.

"As you can see, the dance can't exactly be done in a wheelchair. You get that, right?"

Speechless, Nat didn't know if she should cry or shake her head or nod. She didn't have the guts to do anything. She just sat there, while her brain flooded with the hundreds of times she'd been told, "No, you can't because you're in a wheelchair." No, you can't play softball. No, you can't drive this go-kart. No, you can't be a junior lifeguard. No, you can't skate at my roller-skating birthday party. No. No. No. No.

"This is a good thing!" Calvin continued brightly. "You'll still be in the number, just not doing all the intricate dance stuff. And, hey, less dancing means more acting. Digging into a character of your choice will be essential for you, so I'm glad you're stoked to read the novel."

He waited for Nat to say something, *anything*, so she blurted with as much enthusiasm as she could muster, "Cool."

"You're a true sport," Calvin reflected, placing his *Newsies* cap over his heart. He didn't get it—she *was* a true sport. She was a champion racer. Doing the show without dancing was only going to be a half-step up from a dumb chorus concert. Nat pushed over to her backpack and raced out of the theater as fast as she could.

CHAPTER EIGHT

The Nicest Kids in Town

I can't, I can't, I can't. Outside the JCC, Nat stared with panic at her dad's contact info on her phone. How was she supposed to ask him to pick her up an hour early from rehearsal? What was she supposed to say? *You were right, Dad. One day in, and it's clear: I can't be in the show like everyone else. I quit racing for nothing.*

No. She'd call her mom, and she'd lie. Again.

Nat listened to the phone ring and ring as a fat tear slid down her cheek. She was already on the defensive. *You're overreacting, Mom. It's not a big deal.* Her voicemail kicked in. "Hi, you've reached Amanda Beacon. Please leave your name and number—or lots of numbers!—at the beep." Nat hung up, her screen wet.

She looked behind her as two old ladies exited the JCC, holding green smoothies the color of Elphaba's face. Trying not to let them see her cry, she wiped her eyes and phone with the fringes of her T-shirt, sniffled away the drips in her nose, and tried her dad before she could overthink it.

"Natty," her dad said. "Everything going okay? Play practice is good?"

His voice was full of concern. He knew something was wrong. Of course he knew. "It's called *rehearsal*," Nat corrected. Her voice was quivering so much. "And it's good. Yeah, everything's good."

"Good . . ." her dad said, followed by long, worried silence.

Be peppy like a toy-commercial actor. "So, anyway, rehearsal's over," she said as enthusiastically as she could. "They ended early, so. Do you think you can pick me up?"

"Are you with other kids?" he whispered. "It sounds like you're trying not to sound upset. Say 'seven' if that's true."

Seven. "What? No. I'm alone."

"Oh. Where are the other kids?"

Nat held in a frustrated sigh. "Sometimes we aren't called the whole time. It depends on what they're working on and if we're needed. I'm not needed." She felt a sharp pain in her throat. "So, can you pick me up?"

"I'm finishing up at the DMV. I'm about forty minutes away. That work?"

Nat checked her phone: 4:18. In forty minutes, everyone would be getting out of rehearsal. They'd all see her, a pathetic puddle of tears. If they didn't ignore her, they'd ask her why she'd skipped dance rehearsal. Why she was chilling under the JCC awning all alone.

"Natty, that work?" her dad repeated.

"You can't get here faster?" she blurted, her voice legit cracking now. "What about Mom?"

"Your mom's still at work, and she's not much closer. Why don't I call you an Uber?"

"Um, that's—" Nat's chest started to throb with anxiety. She'd never taken an Uber by herself. What if the car was too high off the ground for her to transfer into? How was she supposed to explain how to put her chair in the trunk? What if the driver didn't want to help her? No. Not happening. "It's fine. I'll just wait for you."

"I'll get there as soon as I can. I swear. I'm—I'm leaving now. Hang tight, okay?"

Nat tried to say more than just "Thanks," but she stopped herself, knowing her voice would shatter. It didn't matter at this point. She was sure her dad was already thinking she'd made a super-stupid mistake in joining the play. It's not like he hadn't warned her.

With nowhere to go and nothing else to do, Nat waited, rewatching funny YouTube videos. Specifically, clips of Broadway's Miscast gala, where famous musical-theater actors sang songs by characters they would never get to play in real life: Guys played girls, girls played guys, old people sang young parts, and young people sang old parts. She started with her favorite clip: three boys around her age performing "The Schuyler Sisters" from *Hamilton*, then moved on to her second favorite: Jeremy Jordan performing "Let It Go" from *Frozen*. She wasn't laughing, but at least she wasn't crying anymore. But thirty seconds into Norbert Leo Butz and Aaron Tveit's rendition of *Wicked*'s hate duet, "What Is This Feeling?" she started to spiral with a tornado of feelings and pressed pause.

Ugh. Normally, she liked watching Miscast, because it gave her hope that one day, when she was a famous actor, she might get miscast as a character like Elphaba—a wicked witch who not only walks but flies! But watching now, Nat realized that the role wouldn't actually be a miscast, at least not in one important way. Elphie had green skin, which totally set her apart from everyone else. Sometimes that was all her Shiz University classmates could see. And Nat had a chair, which totally set her apart. Sometimes, like today, it was all a person could see.

How could Calvin treat her the same way Elphaba was treated? If Broadway Bounders wasn't willing to give her a shot in a musical that was literally about lifting up the different girl, how would *actual* Broadway people be willing to do it? Forget miscasting. Would professionals cast her in *any* role ever?

Feeling totally dejected, Nat shoved her phone into her pocket and stared out at the parking lot until her eyes burned. Then, remembering she had one more option to kill time, she took out the *Wicked* book. Part of her didn't want to think about it right now, but the bigger part of her realized it wasn't the story she was mad at, just the person directing it. She opened to the prologue, "On the Yellow Brick Road," but found herself skipping over Gregory Maguire's adulty words and going straight to Malik's. He'd underlined one of Fiyero's quotes, and next to it he'd written, FIYERO SEES LIFE AS A GIFT BECAUSE OF HIS A+ 'TUDE. *So deep.* On another page, he wrote something less deep, more spoiler alert: FIYERO = MARRIED W/ 3 KIDS B4 ELPHABA?! Was that true?!?!

"Oh, hey, Nat! You're here!"

Nat slammed the book shut. *Malik.* He'd caught her stalking. He was jogging over. His hot-pink bandanna was dark pink now, soaked with sweat, and he smelled like tangy citrus. He'd probably eaten an orange. Or he smelled like fruit after a workout. *Don't ask him which.*

"You started already?" he asked.

"Started?"

"The book," he said, pointing at it in her lap.

"Oh, I wasn't really . . . I was just flipping."

"Cool, cool."

Nat watched his nose crinkle with curiosity. He was about to ask her why she'd ditched dance rehearsal; she knew it.

"Want a pretzel?" he asked instead.

"A what?" *You know what a pretzel is.*

Malik slung his drawstring backpack to his shoulder, pulled out a half-eaten bag of honey twists, and offered it to her. "I've got, like, five left."

Nat wasn't sure if he'd said five so she wouldn't greedily take more than one or if five was a high number and she should help herself. "Thanks," she said with a small chuckle, modestly taking a broken one.

Malik held out a full twist and tapped it against hers, like a grown-up sword and a baby sword. "Cheers," he said.

Nat nibbled her pretzel. They ate in nice, crunchy silence. Finally, the crunching silence died, and she looked at the door. Not because she wanted other kids to join them, but she was wondering where they were. "How come you're out before everyone else?" she asked, then realized he could ask her the same thing.

"Calvin called the end of rehearsal, and then . . . groups. *You know.*"

She didn't.

"Everyone's so slow. Fig had to go to the bathroom, and Savannah had to fix her hair, and Hudson had to change into flip-flops. So, I was like, 'Peace. I'll meet you all outside.' It's really hot in there."

"It's really hot out here, too."

"True. I forgot it's, like, *summer* summer."

"I'm totally a summer person, though," Nat said.

Malik squinted. "Your birthday is August twenty-fourth."

"No, ha. It's December—"

"Don't tell me! Seventeenth. No, fourteenth. You're a Sagittarius. I can feel it in my bones." Malik cracked a knuckle, and the smell of citrus jumped into Nat's nose. She suddenly wanted to take his hand in hers. "You're a dream chaser, Nat. I can tell."

"How do you know?"

"Because I'm one, too. December nineteenth."

"December sixteenth! Birthday twins! Almost!" Nat clapped. "We were probably babies in the hospital at the same time, but, like, in different parts of the country."

"That's so funny to think about." Now Malik looked at the door, hopefully because there was laughter leaking out and not because he wanted their alone time to end. She shouldn't have applauded herself. "Hey, how come *you're* out here?" he asked, gazing back at her.

And . . . there was the question. Nat half shrugged. *How could I not have thought through an answer in the last FORTY MINUTES?!* "It's, uh, complicated."

"MY FIY-FIY!" Savannah suddenly shouted at Malik as she burst through the JCC doors.

Malik shook his head. "Nuh-uh. Not callin' you—"

"Not calling me what?" Savannah asked coyly, skipping to him and grabbing his hand. She gave him a series of low fives. "Hello, Fiy-Fiy? Not calling me *what*?"

Malik playfully rolled his eyes. "Glin-Glin."

"YOU JUST DID!" Savannah screamed.

Nat retreated into herself, wishing she didn't have to watch them flirt. She guessed it made sense, though. He was

Fiyero. She was Glinda. They had to have chemistry onstage. It was probably best for the show that they have chemistry offstage, too.

Miraculously, the rest of the cast began pouring out of the JCC, and Malik got distracted. He shouted, "Bye, guys! See you tomorrow!" and "Bring more Popchips, Marti, please!" and "Yo, Avi. Send your cat my regards." Meanwhile, the other Oz Bounderz were springing toward them: sweaty, exhausted messes. Hudson fanned his red, freckly face with his libretto. Rey retied her long black hair into a topknot. Jaclyn dragged her skateboard. Fig collapsed onto the concrete like a dead body. "Chalk my outline," he said. "I'm not getting up."

"The ground is germy," Savannah warned, throwing an arm over Malik's shoulders. She immediately retracted it, flapping like an injured bird. "Ew, omigod, omigod. You were not this sweaty two minutes ago. What happened?!"

"Chill, it's water," Malik said.

"Jesus Christ Superstar."

"Kidding. It's sweat."

While everyone cracked up, Savannah smacked Malik's shoulder. "*Seeeee?*" she whined to the group, but mostly Nat. "Boys are the mostest grossest."

Hudson cleared his throat. "Not *only* boys. Remember when Jac licked her skateboard wheel?"

"It was a dare!" Jaclyn protested. "And Fig's way sweatier than Malik."

Nat watched Fig squat over the sweat imprint of his body like a detective. "Death by dancing," he said, stroking an invisible mustache.

"Ha. Ha. Can we go, *pleaaaase*?" Hudson whined. "I need AC and fried pickles STAT."

"Fried pickles?" Rey asked incredulously. "This isn't, like, fancy Manhattan."

"You're telling me that there are no Applebee's in Manhattan?"

"Not with fried pickles on their menu, there aren't."

Nat took in the group and felt a pinch of exclusion. They'd all just danced together. They were all fighting exhaustion together. Clearly, they were all about to go to Applebee's together.

"I don't eat fried food," Savannah announced, then looked at Nat. "Do you?"

"Sometimes, yeah," Nat admitted. "I've never had a fried pickle, though."

BEEP! BEEP! Right in front of her was her dad in their green Nissan Altima. She put up her finger to tell him, "Just a sec," but he was already out of the car and making his way toward the trunk, getting it ready for her chair. She guessed it was for the best, anyway. She didn't want to go through the humiliation of getting left on the curb.

"Come!" Malik exclaimed suddenly. "Come to Applebee's!"

Nat took a second to see who he was talking to. Her. He was talking to her. "Me?"

"Duh," Savannah said. "We're literally standing in a circle around you."

Nat felt herself light up from the inside out. *Applebee's, here I come!* But then her brain got flooded with all the obstacles she'd have to face—asking her dad for permission, asking her dad for a ride there and back, asking her dad for money—and the light started to dim. "How do you get there?" she asked.

"We, uh, walk," Malik said. "It's not far at all. Like ten minutes."

"Just ask your dad," Rey said, looking over Nat's shoulder. "Maybe he can drive you?"

"I don't need a ride if . . ." Nat turned around, and her dad was, *oh God,* coming over. But, luckily, before he could reach the sidewalk, the *Rocky* theme song erupted from his gym shorts and he took a phone call back by the trunk of the car.

"You should let Malik talk to your dad," Savannah insisted. "Parents always say yes to him. My mom's, like, obsessed with him."

"He puts them under a spell," Fig added, waggling an eyebrow with impressive control.

"Dude," Malik protested. "I'm polite and respectful. It's not that hard."

"For a parent charmer," Fig said, then broke into a chant. "*Ma-lik! Ma-lik! Ma-lik!*"

Nat tried to cut in, "Hey, it's—*I* can just ask my dad—!" But everyone quickly joined in, chanting over her. "*Ma-lik Young! Ma-lik Young! Ma-lik Young!*"

Nat wanted to curl up and hide behind the hedges of the JCC. First of all, Chloe was her only friend who talked to her dad. He would probably freak out if a random boy asked to take his daughter out to dinner.

"Ma-lik Young, yeah! Ma-lik Young, yeah!"

Second of all, he'd be majorly confused. Nat had *just* called him, upset. He'd probably assume she was getting peer-pressured. Or worse, that she couldn't handle the ups and downs of being in a show.

"Ma-lik Young! Fi-ye-ro! Ma-lik Young! Fi-ye-ro!"

"Fine," Malik said. "I'll do it."

The group screamed in celebration. If Nat didn't know what he'd agreed to, she'd think he was about to slay a dragon or something.

"Nat, do you *want* me to talk to your dad?" Malik asked.

Not really? "Sure, yeah," Nat replied, feeling her cheeks burn. "I'll come, though, so he's not totally weirded out. Not that it's weird."

"I get it; it's cool."

Then, just like that, Malik followed Nat to her dad. Just the two of them.

"Wait! I'm coming, too!" Savannah called, racing after them.

Just the *three* of them. Nat turned the trunk's corner first. "Hey, Dad?"

"Natty, what *happened* in there?" he asked, hanging up and dropping his phone into his pocket. "Do you need me to go inside and talk to the director?"

And . . . she should never have called him. "I'm fine, it's fine," she said, giving him *Please don't blow this for me* eyes. He wasn't really looking at her eyes, though, because Malik and Savannah, two of the coolest-looking kids ever, were suddenly flanking her. "Dad, this is Malik and Savannah," she said stiffly. "They're going to Applebee's."

Without hesitation, Malik put out his hand for a shake. "Hey, Mr. Beacon. I'm Malik. I'm in the show with Nat." Her dad made one of his impressed "Hmgh" sounds and shook back. "I don't know if you guys have dinner already planned, but can Nat join us? My cousin is a server there on her summer breaks from college, so we get a sick discount."

"You've got a hookup," Nat's dad said. "Totally *sick*."

"We won't eat ANY fried food," Savannah blurted over him, thankfully.

"Oh, I'm not concerned about that," he said with a dad-chuckle, even though he campaigned against fried food with the gusto that other parents campaigned against vaping. "I'm concerned about—" He glanced at Nat's wheelchair. "It's been a long day. For me, for Nat . . ."

"It's a short walk," Malik pressed. "And Applebee's has a ramp. We all have your daughter's back. We really want her to come."

Nat's dad made his impressed "Hmgh" sound again and looked at Nat.

"I do. I definitely want to go." She was trying not to blush.

Malik went on. "Going out after the first rehearsal is kind of a tradition. We always have so much to talk about."

"So much," Savannah said in agreement.

Nat watched her dad hesitate. He looked at Malik and then at Savannah. "Okay," he finally said. Though there were still questions behind his eyes: *You'll help my daughter wheel up hills? You're not going to take any grassy shortcuts?*

"Dad! It's totally fine," Nat said with conviction.

As it turned out, everything *was* fine. Her dad slipped her a twenty, and she and the Oz Bounderz strolled down a main street with a wide, smooth sidewalk, then made a left into the parking lot of a shopping center. There was an easy short ramp that brought her right inside the restaurant. Malik's cousin, Eternity, brought over nachos and their Classic Combo on the house: wings, spinach and artichoke dip, chicken quesadillas, and mozzarella sticks. Everyone was stuffing their faces and rehashing funny moments from rehearsal, like when Malik accidentally read Savannah's line instead of his own. And when, in character, Hudson asked

Rey to the Ozdust Dance and Rey went off script to tell him, "Nah, bruh." And when, during music practice, Fig had sung Jaclyn's part in his falsetto.

After that, Savannah asked what Nat had hoped everyone had forgotten. "So, Nat, why'd you disappear from rehearsal?" The question sat there on top of the nachos, sinking in queso.

"Oh, yeah," Malik said. "What happened? Your dad seemed worried."

Nat nudged a chicken wing across her plate, going quiet. So everyone else got quiet, too. Which was noticeable in the baby-crying, big-bash madness that was Applebee's on a summer night. "So, I didn't really *want* to leave," Nat started slowly. "Like, I wanted to learn the dance."

"You couldn't get onstage?" Rey asked in a panic. "Oh God—I'm the worst—I wasn't there to help you get onstage."

Nat gave her a reassuring smile. "No, no, it's not that at all. Calvin told me I could go home. That the dance can't be done in a wheelchair. Which, I guess, technically, he's right about. But I don't get why he couldn't let me try to do it my own way." She took a strained breath. "I can do stuff. I wheelchair race competitively. I'm an athlete. I don't get why he couldn't give me a chance."

"I dunno," Malik said. "That's messed up."

"Yeah, he could have *asked* you," Fig said.

"Did you say something?" Jaclyn asked.

"No, but I wish I had." Nat sighed. "The news came really fast. On the inside, I was like, 'Wait, whaaaaa?' But on the outside, I was like— I don't know how to describe it."

"Stuck?" Malik offered.

"Actually, yeah," Nat said, a little surprised. "I was *so* excited to get into the show. I still am. But now I feel like I was half-cast, you know? It's frustrating to have the director, someone I'm supposed to *trust*, just tell me what I can't do."

Savannah dramatically dropped a mozzarella stick on her plate. "Omigod, I know what you can do to get more involved!" she declared. "You can be Rey's teacher. Like, an independent study! You can tell her what she can and can't do as Nessarose, so she can portray her realistically!!!"

Nat sucked in a breath between her teeth. She liked Rey, a lot actually, but that didn't mean she wanted to be her wheelchair consultant. She wanted to be a part of the musical fully, like every other cast member. If not as Nessarose, then at least as an ensemble member who moved.

Meanwhile, the group had gone quiet again. Rey was cringing. Hudson was squinting with horror. Everyone else had *This is awkward* expressions.

"What?" Savannah asked, her back sinking into the booth's cushion. "Was that offensive?"

Hudson straight-up nodded. Then he stopped and looked at Nat. "Actually, was it?"

"It's not that," Nat said with a half chuckle, then looked at Rey. "I'll totally help you. It'll be cool to show everyone what people in wheelchairs are capable of; it's just that . . ."

"It doesn't solve the problem," Hudson said, completing her thought. "The character of Nessarose has her own track. Calvin's seen *Wicked* on Broadway. He knows how to teach her blocking. But he clearly doesn't know how his ensemble choreography will work for Nat."

"Yeah, exactly," Nat said.

"So, what *would* solve the problem?" Savannah asked.

Nat slurped her Pepsi as everyone stared at her, waiting. She knew what to say, but she was worried about saying it, since it required a pretty generous volunteer.

"We could talk to Calvin for you," Jaclyn suggested.

"Thanks, but . . ." She twirled her straw around the ice at the bottom of her glass. *Say it, say it.* "I think I have to *show* Calvin. Like, dance for him to a *Wicked* song. Which means someone's got to teach me what I missed—"

"YOU AND ME!" Hudson yelped without letting a nanosecond pass. "How's tomorrow after rehearsal? I can come over and run through the moves, and like you said, you can try to do them in your own way."

Nat felt the corners of her mouth shoot up into a smile. "I think it's called translating," she said, remembering one of her Zoomers friends using the word to talk about ballet. "You can help me *translate* the dance."

"Perfect. And then when we're ready, like, after the retreat, we can show Calvin and Cora what we've worked on."

"The retreat?" Nat asked.

Savannah slammed her palms on the table. "You don't KNOW about the RETREAT? It's the BEST WEEKEND EVER. We go to this campsite and rehearse and bond and swim and do life-changing stuff."

"It's not this weekend, but the next," Rey chimed in.

"So, by then," Hudson said, "we should be all set with the dance." He narrowed his eyebrows. "Nobody puts Natty in a corner!"

Nat broke out laughing. She couldn't believe he'd just referenced one of her favorite old-timey movies, *Dirty Dancing*. Nat didn't know any other kid who'd seen it. Being a dancer, of course Hudson had.

"You dig the plan?" Hudson asked.

Digging it deeper than deep, Nat threw back a nacho—*crunch, crunch, grin.* "Let's show Calvin what we've got."

NatThrowinAwayMyShot + GoChloGo

NatThrowinAwayMyShot: Chlo!! It's been bananas here!

NatThrowinAwayMyShot: Chlo?

GoChloGo: Hi

NatThrowinAwayMyShot: The cast is sooo cool. Rey's really sporty and confident. Savannah's prob gonna be famous one day. Fig is the funniest. Actually Jac is. Hudson is my hero. And Malik . . . just aaaaaaaah! I've never had a crush b4 like this. He obv only likes me as a friend, but still!!!!

GoChloGo: Cool

NatThrowinAwayMyShot: Yup! So, what's going on with u?

GoChloGo: Can't talk 2 much longer. Heading 2 park.

NatThrowinAwayMyShot: For the program you're doing?

GoChloGo: No, with Beatrice to hang out 😆

NatThrowinAwayMyShot: Haha, what?!

GoChloGo: Y r u haha-ing?

NatThrowinAwayMyShot: Beatrice Chu?

GoChloGo: uh huh

NatThrowinAwayMyShot: So random! Whyyyy?

GoChloGo: Gotta go, talk tomorrow?

NatThrowinAwayMyShot: Hudson's coming over to do choreo 😆

NatThrowinAwayMyShot: But after that? Or the next day?

NatThrowinAwayMyShot: Luv ya, have fun!

CHAPTER NINE

One Step Closer

DING DONG, THE WITCH IS DEAD! the doorbell sang.

"HUDSON'S HERE!" Nat screamed in her head at the same time that her mom, unfortunately, screamed it out loud. Nat dashed toward the door. So did her mom. So did Warbucks. "I got it," Nat said, twisting the knob. There stood Hudson, balancing on his shoulder a tote bag of dance shoes.

"Hey!" Nat said.

"Hey!" Hudson overlapped. "Can I steal your doorbell? Mine's a boring intercom thing that buzzes."

"Riiight?"

"Come on in, Hudson," Nat's mom said in her overeager-hostess voice. Hudson stepped inside, and Warbucks went nuts, treating him to a slobber facial. "Warbucks, chill!" she scolded.

"Did you say 'Warbucks'?" Hudson asked, wiping his face with the bottom of his sequined tank top. "As in, Daddy Warbucks?"

"Yeah, exactly!" Nat said. "*Annie* reference what-what!"

Nat's mom led Warbucks out the back door to the yard, calling over her shoulder, "Hudson, do you want anything to drink? Eat?" Her pitch rose. "I can make cookies! Oatmeal raisin, sugar, whatever!" Her pitch rose again. "I'm Amanda, by the way—Nat's mom. Not sister! Ha! Ha!"

"I think my granola bar will hold me over," Hudson called back. "But thanks!"

"Well, you just let me or Nat know. We're so glad you were willing to come over."

Ouch. "So. My room?" Nat asked.

"Sure," Hudson replied.

Nat led Hudson to her bedroom and clicked her door closed. She self-consciously rolled toward him as he caressed the furry blanket at the foot of her bed. She needed him to know that he didn't have to stay long, really. He was doing her a big favor. "Look, we don't have to—"

"Girls' beds are the best beds." He sighed, back-flopping onto her comforter. "My bed's boring. It's just gray and stiff."

"You can get one of those foam eggcrate things," Nat suggested.

"Maybe I'll ask for a feather top for my birthday, even though I'm sure I'll just get a lacrosse stick."

"Definitely don't sleep on a lacrosse stick."

"Pfff, ow. I'd be like the princess from the musical *Once Upon a Mattress*."

Nat didn't know that one. "Totally," she said anyway.

Hudson butt-bounced off the bed and pointed at a picture on Nat's desk of Nat and Chloe at the beach, wearing ridiculous straw summer hats and reading *Popstar!* "Who's that?" he asked.

"Chloe," Nat replied. "My best friend from home."

"Do you miss her?"

She nodded thoughtfully. Of course she missed her. Just saying Chloe's name aloud gave her a pang of heartache. But at the same time, the two of them seemed to be doing a lot better without each other than she'd imagined they would.

"What—did something happen between you two?"

"Oh! No, not at all," Nat said. "I miss Chloe a ton, and nothing can replace our friendship. But I guess since I've been here, hanging out with you and the other Broadway Bounders has kind of filled that hole."

"Wow."

"Sorry." Nat cringed. "That's weird. You're right—we basically just met."

"No, God—I wasn't thinking that!" Hudson plopped down on the floor beside her. "I was thinking about how I felt the same way when I joined Broadway Bounders. I didn't move across the country or anything, but I had, like, zero friends in elementary school. Kids called me pretty horrible names, but at the JCC, I basically found my people after the first rehearsal."

"The same people you're friends with now?"

"The same people *we're* friends with now."

Nat gave him a *You really didn't have to say that* look.

"I mean it, even though it's a really dorky thing for me to say." He pressed his lips together, then smacked his mouth open. "It's almost as dorky as that," he said, pointing to the bulletin board behind Nat, where she'd pinned the *Wicked* audition flyer and acceptance email.

Busted. "Oh, ha."

"Don't worry, I have it on my wall, too. The flyer, not the email, though."

Nat laughed, and a tangle of nerves seemed to drop from her shoulders. "*Wicked* was the first musical I ever auditioned for, so. I dunno, I like putting feel-good stuff up on my wall."

"So I see," Hudson teased, taking in all the framed inspirational quotes.

"Ooh!" Nat said, suddenly smacked with an idea. "I should record all the funny stuff that happens in rehearsal and make a quote wall!"

"We already have a secret one backstage, behind a shelf of prop clocks. So far, no one in charge has noticed the vandalism."

"You have to show me!"

"Duh. And once Cora designs the show poster—she always designs it—you should get the entire cast to sign it and hang it up in your room, too." Hudson kneeled, sandwiching Nat's cheeks with his palms. "Okay. Enough talking. Let's DANCE THROUGH LIFE!"

"Yes, let's!" Nat replied messily, her lips puckered out.

Earlier, Nat's mom had helped Nat transform her room into a "dance studio." Basically, she'd shoved the bed into a corner, exposing more hardwood-floor space in front of the mirrored closets. Nat connected her phone to her Bluetooth speaker and cued up "Dancing Through Life."

Hudson broke into a lungey stretch. "Let me show you the first few eight-counts we learned," he suggested. "Then we can start to *translate*."

"Nice word," Nat said.

"I listen," Hudson replied with a bow.

The music blasted, and Hudson faced Nat. He tapped his foot and mouthed the counts. Then he began to turn and leap and jump and arm-wave with the grace of a butterfly. He grabbed Nat's plush heart-shaped pillow and used it as a makeshift dance partner. Somehow, he made the pillow come to life, too, dipping it and lifting it and twirling it. "That's it," he said, striking a final pose with jazz hands.

"Oh, yeah, that's it," Nat joked. "I swear, I'm more out of breath just watching you."

"I'm out of breath!" he protested, breathing normally. "Okay, let's break it down. The first move is a half turn.

We all face upstage with our backs to the audience. Then we turn front."

"Great." Nat turned her back to the mirror.

"So, we're going to turn on the count of three, land on four." He snapped four times to set the rhythm, then jumped in. "One, two, THREE, FOUR!"

Before Nat had even gripped her wheels, Hudson was facing the mirror. "So . . . I definitely need more time to turn."

Hudson squinted in thought. "Maybe have your hands on your wheels earlier? Like, can you start turning on two?"

"Sure, yeah. I'll try."

"Cool." He snapped out the rhythm again. "One, TWO—"

Nat started pushing, and by the time Hudson got to four, she was facing front.

"YAAAAS!" he called, rushing in for a high five. "Your chair equals awesome."

Awesome, awesome, awesome. The word bounced around in Nat's head. She'd never heard kids call her chair anything before. Normally, they talked around it, avoiding her, like they were both invisible. "Wanna try?" she blurted.

"Try what? Your chair?"

Say never mind. "Yeah. Is that stupid?" *Yes. Stop talking.* "It's just that I have an extra one in the garage."

"Um. That would be SO COOL."

"Ha! Oh, okay! G-great," Nat stuttered, dizzy with shock. Wild, excited shock. She pushed as fast as she could to the kitchen. "Mom! Can you please bring in Eliza?"

"Uh, sure!" her mom said, slamming her laptop shut and running to the garage.

Hudson arrived at the kitchen table beside Nat. "Please tell me you named your wheelchair after Eliza Schuyler Hamilton, my dream role."

"MY dream role!" Nat squealed.

"OUR dream role!" he squealed back. "OMIGOD, I'M OBSESSED!"

Nat grabbed two water bottles from the fridge and tossed Hudson one. He caught it with his left hand. "So, the chair you're sitting in now, does she also have a name?"

"Of course. This is Peaches. Named after her pink color and also the funky new orphan in *Annie Warbucks*, the *Annie* sequel."

"So, one chair's an orphan, the other founded an orphanage?"

"I never thought of it that way, but yeah!"

Nat's mom wheeled in Eliza, which was purple with silver and gold splashes of paint. She parked her in front of Hudson. "You two talk so fast I can hardly understand a word you're saying."

"I didn't realize, did you?" Nat asked Hudson, laughing a little.

"Yes," he replied, prompting her to crack up even more. He carefully lowered his butt into the chair. "I'm nervous. You maneuver it like it's a part of your body. I'm gonna suck."

Nat shook her head. "You have, like, the most perfect control when you dance. It'll be no different in the chair."

"I dunno . . ." He gripped the wheels for dear life. "Okay, okay, now what?"

Nat bumped her eyebrows. "Relax and follow me!" She began pushing back toward her bedroom. "Oh, mind the bend!" She took the first corner, pulling back on her right wheel.

Suddenly, there was a crash!

"God, sorry!" Hudson exclaimed.

"You okay?!" Nat asked, turning around as Hudson wheeled himself away from the wall.

"Yup. I'm good. Wall's good. Eliza's judging me."

Nat chuckled with relief. "Eliza doesn't judge; trust me! Though if she were judging anyone, it would be me for not actually explaining what to do when there's a bend." Her eyes met Hudson's eyes, and she wasn't even craning her neck. It was nice. She was never at eye level with her friends. "It's harder than it looks, I guess."

"Ch'yeah."

Back in Nat's room and in front of the mirror, she coached Hudson as he practiced the first turn in the choreography.

"Do I push the actual tire or the metal pushing part?" he asked.

"I sometimes push a little bit of both. Pro-tip: Use the metal push rim, but when you need to get as much momentum as possible, put your hand over both the rubber tire *and* the push rim."

Hudson went for it, starting the turn on three and landing well past five. Plus, he totally used his legs.

"Closer, but try not to cheat."

"Ah, it's so hard!" he said, burying his face in his hands. "I feel like I need to record you and then watch it back in slow motion."

"You can totally record—" Nat sprang forward. "Oh! Do you know the Rollettes?"

"Is that a girl band?"

"They're a dance group. They're all beautiful girls in their twenties who are in wheelchairs. They do big numbers and also make music videos."

Hudson tossed his arms up. "Seriously? You're telling me this *now*?"

Nat laughed a "Sorry!" then pulled up the Rollettes' first-ever dance competition. It was at International Cheer Union with lead dancer and founder Chelsie Hill. "You see how she does a wheelie?" Nat asked. "And a dip?"

"Yes, I see it!"

"The way she moves, the way they all do—it's with complete confidence. They own their bodies."

"Plus, they're really strong and hot."

"Ugh," Nat said. "I wish I could be that amazing."

Hudson scoffed. "You can be, are you kidding? When you dance for Calvin, his head is going to pirouette off his neck."

"Morbid. I love it."

Nat and Hudson rehearsed some upper-body-focused moves, which were a lot simpler to translate, and then it was time for the partner work. Nat tossed him a fuzzy pink pillow from her bed, but he tossed it right back onto her comforter. "We've got each other, right?" he asked.

"Yeah," Nat answered, "but only one of us will be in a chair."

"Touché," he said. "I'll take that pillow back for now. Then once we figure out the steps and timing, I'll partner with you out of the chair."

Nat kept her eyes glued to a random flower on her comforter as the word "partner" danced around in her head. As a certain *someone* danced around in her head.

"Grab a pillow for yourself, too," Hudson added.

"God, I wish I could dance with Malik," Nat blurted.

"Me too."

Pillow drop. Nat turned around faster than she had in the past hour. "Wait. Omigod. *Seriously?*" she asked.

"I mean, I'm kind of joking. But you're serious?"

"Yeah. I mean, *yeah*! He's really cute and he's so nice—"

"And talented and philosophical and a lot of other very good adjectives."

Nat smirked at Hudson, and Hudson smirked back. They rolled toward each other, slowly, as Nat's brain turned into a hurricane of questions. "Is he gay?" she asked.

"I wish."

"Is there something going on between him and Savannah?"

"She's always liked him."

"And he's always liked her?"

"Everyone's been waiting for him to get the hint."

"How do you know he hasn't already gotten the hint?"

"Because boys are stupid with stuff like that."

"So, do you think he'll like her back when he realizes she likes him?"

"I dunno, probably."

Nat's heart sank to the pit of her stomach.

"If he were smart, though," Hudson said, "he'd like you back."

Nat's heart bobbed up, and there was a knock at the door. "Honey, it's me!" her mom said, creaking it open. Nat half expected her to come in with a platter of Pinterest-inspired *Wicked* cookies, but instead she brought the news that Hudson's dad was here to pick him up.

"Nooooo!" Hudson moaned. "I'll text him 'five more minutes.' He'll understand, right?"

"Right," Nat overlapped with her mom.

Left alone together, Hudson rose from Eliza and grabbed his tote bag of dance shoes he'd never ended up using. "Maybe we can make this a thing?"

Yes! "Are you sure?" Nat asked casually, shoving a clump of damp curls behind her ear. "I know it's a lot to have to help the cast all day and then help me."

"Stahhp, it was so fun."

Nat smiled, then swallowed hard. "Also, thanks for sharing so much stuff with me today. If it helps, I got called a lot of names in elementary school, too. *And* middle school. People don't always see me. They see the chair."

"Their loss, honestly. Oh!" He clapped two tap shoes together. "You should make *everyone* get in Eliza! It should be a worldwide requirement!"

"Ha," Nat said. "Unfortunately, most people act scared of my chair." She looked at the emailed cast list behind Hudson's head. "Like, even in *Wicked.* Your Munchkin character, Boq. He has a crush on Glinda, but Glinda makes him ask out Nessarose as a form of charity, just because she's in a wheelchair. Is it so crazy for Boq to actually love Nessa, but not crazy for Fiyero to love Glinda or even Elphaba? Like, what?!"

Hudson blinked in astonishment. "You're right. You're totally right."

"One day, I would love to play a lead. Not give advice to an actor playing a role in a chair. Not play a lead character in a chair. But, like, play a legit, normal leading lady. Maybe even one with love stuff."

"I want that for you, too. Like, that NEEDS to happen." Hudson went suddenly quiet, tucking the tap shoes into his tote. "Obviously, it's not the same for me, but . . . Okay, I'm just going to say it. I like being a dance captain, but I don't want to be stuck on the sidelines helping Malik forever. For once, I want to be the lead, too."

Nat wheeled a step closer. "You should be. You'd be amazing."

"Thanks," Hudson said. "I mean, I get it. I'm not the hottest manly person or whatever. But I can act. I can *play* a leading guy role. Or a leading girl role. A leading role, period. Willing suspension of disbelief, people!"

"Wait, remind me," Nat said. "What does that mean, exactly?"

"I think it can mean a lot of things?" Hudson began to pace between the bed and the bathroom door. "What *I* mean, though, is that when people come to see theater, they know it's not real. So, if an actor is playing a character that doesn't fit the character's body or voice or type perfectly, it's fine. The audience accepts it."

Nat's favorite musicals swirled around in her brain as she fantasized about Miscast being not just an annual gala but a thing that happened all the time. "Omigod, *Hamilton*!" she blurted out.

"What about it?"

"The whole show is like a giant willing suspension of disbelief because they cast people of color as the Founding Fathers!"

"Oh, yeah! You're right!"

Nat started to pace, too. "I just feel like theater is the one place where we can try on different roles and show the world that there's more to us than what people might see."

"Especially when the actor is talented. I think talent outweighs any 'distraction.'"

"True. That's totally—" Nat sprang forward again as something clicked. "Hudson! 'Willing suspension of disbelief'! That's our quote for the secret wall backstage!"

"YAAAAAASSSSSSSS!" He clasped her hands in his and began jumping up and down, which morphed into a sort of Irish step dance.

BEEEEEEEEEEP!

"Shoot, I never texted my dad!" Hudson threw his arms around Nat's neck for a goodbye. He held the hug. Their hearts were touching—beating together, Nat could swear.

"Thanks, Amanda slash Nat's Mom-Not-Sister! See you tomorrow!" he hollered on the way out. It reverberated around the house with such fervor, it put their doorbell to shame.

OZ BOUNDERZ

TheSoundOfMalik: Who's pumped for tomorrow's retreat?!

LegallySavannah: Meeeee ♥

PurpleHairyPoppins: Wicked good time, yee-haw!

JACLYNandHYDE: Wicked = NOT a western LOLZ

PurpleHairyPoppins: Wicked Witch of the WEST

NatThrowinAwayMyShot: What did u pack? I feel like I'm missing stuff.

JACLYNandHYDE: Don't underestimate the value of bug spray

TheReyWhereItHappens: Bathing suit, water bottle, bra, underwear, extra marshmallows, travel toiletries, flashlight, socks, sneakers, flip flops, sweatshirt, script

DearEvanHudson: Ha, bra

TheReyWhereItHappens: I copied + pasted my list. ¯_(ツ)_/¯

TheSoundOfMalik: Bring your portable speakers, Fig

PurpleHairyPoppins: On it

TheReyWhereItHappens: SLEEPING BAG! Yikes, I forgot to include sleeping bag!

NatThrowinAwayMyShot: Oh no . . . I don't have one.

TheReyWhereItHappens: I'll bring my sister's for u

NatThrowinAwayMyShot: ah, thank u!!!

LegallySavannah: Ladies, I have a white noise machine and sleep masks 4 us

PurpleHairyPoppins: Someone bring fly tape. I still have the one from last summer.

DearEvanHudson: Ew, with all the dead flies???

PurpleHairyPoppins: Let's hope they're dead.

CHAPTER TEN

Waving Through a Window

"DAD, COME ON!" Nat hollered down the hall. "WE'RE GOING TO BE LATE!" She checked her phone. 10:14 AM. It was an eleven-minute drive to the JCC. It would take her an extra two minutes to transfer in and out of the car. The bus was supposed to leave the JCC at 10:30 AM sharp. They were cutting it stupidly close.

"All right, all right," her dad said, rushing to the empty key rack.

"I got you," Nat said, tossing him the car keys. "Let's get the show on the road!"

Staring out the front windshield, Nat's brain worked in overdrive. *Has Hudson saved me a seat? Maybe, but what if Malik wants to sit next to me? Hudson would understand, and he'd have Rey. But what if Rey wants to sit next to me?! She doesn't know I like-like Malik, so maybe she wouldn't understand. Ahhhhh!*

Nat and her dad pulled into the JCC parking lot thirteen torturous minutes later. The bus was parked outside the front entrance. Nat spotted Hudson climbing in, with Rey right behind him. Savannah was on the curb, yanking Malik away from Fig. Her hair was in a perfectly messy ponytail, and she was sporting sandals right out of a Greek warrior movie. Nat looked down at her pink Timberlands. She'd worn them as a camping accessory, but maybe that was silly.

Nat transferred into Peaches with a nervous thud. While her dad went to park, she wheeled to Lulu, who was holding a clipboard and checking off the names of kids as they boarded the bus. "Natalie! You're here!" she exclaimed, her arched eyebrows falling into a furrow. "Okay."

Nat followed Lulu's gaze to the back of the bus. "Yeah, is everything—?" She cut herself off. There was NO LIFT IN SIGHT. *No. No. No. No.* Nat's heart began pounding so hard, so instantly, it clogged her ears. "What—what happened?" she croaked.

"I requested a wheelchair accessible bus," Lulu replied, pressing her hand to her forehead. "Nat, I swear I did. I even called to confirm."

How many times? Confirming once meant nothing. Confirming twice meant something. Confirming three times was the only way to get what you wanted when it came to accessibility.

"Anyway, it's broken," Lulu carried on. "The bus I requested had some issues, so they sent this one instead. But of course, it's not what we ordered. It's just a *hiccup*, but . . ."

Lulu kept talking, but between Nat's pounding heart and the cast's disorganized singing of the cult musical *Be More Chill*, she didn't hear a word. She wanted to be inside the bus, with everyone else, belting along to "I Love Play Rehearsal." Not outside, baking in the sun and getting barraged with bad news.

"What's up?" Nat's dad asked, positioning himself between Nat and Lulu. Since Nat was busy staring into the bus windows, looking for her friends, Lulu stuttered a response. "Well, this bus—it arrived—and, well, it's not—"

"Can they bring an accessible bus instead?" he asked.

"No, it's broken," Nat answered.

Nat's dad sighed. "We both know those lifts are about as reliable as my BlackBerry. So. Nat, what do you want to do? You want me to carry you on?"

Nat cringed. "No, because then who is going to get me off?"

Lulu half raised her hand, but Nat ignored it. No way was she going to be carried in like a baby.

"Right," Nat's dad said. "Well, we can just follow the bus."

"It's a two-hour drive," Lulu warned. "Are you sure? That's a long way."

They both looked at Nat.

If the man wants to drive me, let him drive me! Nat fell into a quiet panic. Her body and voice were powering off, even though her brain was on fire. Her dad shouldn't have to drive her. She was promised by Cora that the entire trip would be accessible. If the first step—*getting there*—wasn't assessible, how was she supposed to trust that the rest of it would be?

"Hey, not to worry! I got you," Nat's dad said, placing a trembling hand on Nat's shoulder. Actually, the trembling was all her.

Meanwhile, Lulu pressed her hand to her cheek, like she was trying out a theatrical gesture for distress. "You know, Nat," she said, "if you want to bring someone in the car with you, that would be just fine."

It was suddenly *her* responsibility to find a companion. As if this whole transportation snafu was *her* fault. Her eyes burning, she scanned the bus once more, looking for Hudson, Rey, Malik, anyone who might not mind accompanying her. But she only saw Savannah, her head out an open window, tanning, wearing enormous, circular white sunglasses. She looked like she was shooting a commercial for Coca-Cola.

"Hey, Savannah!" Nat called, pushing toward the rear of the bus.

Savannah jerked her head toward Nat, her sunglasses falling down the bridge of her nose. "Yeah?" she asked.

"Want to ride with me and my dad?"

"Omigod, whaaaa?" she said, then ducked her head back into the bus and shut the window. She was resting her head on someone's shoulder. *Malik's shoulder.* Nat waited a second, hoping Malik might notice her and pop his head out next, but like the rest of the cast, he was absorbed in singing.

Nat turned away from the bus. The burning in her eyes intensified, and before she could will herself to keep it together, she became a puddle of tears. Her nose got stuffed up, and her cheeks got blotchy, and she'd never felt so self-conscious.

Her dad rushed over and kissed her head. "Meet you there," he called to Lulu, then shepherded Nat to the car.

Sitting in the passenger seat, Nat held in a sob. *How can I show my parents I can do more, when stuff like this keeps happening to me?!*

"Natty. It's okay. I'm telling you: This is just a little hiccup."

"IT'S NOT JUST A HICCUP! THIS IS MY LIFE!"

The bus started to roll out. She could hear the chants, "WICKED *RETREAT! HEY!* WICKED *RETREAT!*" and could see, through the emergency back door, all the fists pumping.

Her dad put his hand out, and Nat reluctantly put her hand in his. He squeezed. "Nat, tell me honestly. You definitely want to go?"

No. "Yeah."

"How's this? I'll drive, and you just know that we can turn around at any point."

Now Nat worried that Savannah wouldn't be the only one who ignored her. She worried the activities wouldn't be accessible. She worried about where she'd sleep and who might help her. But she also worried that she was worrying her dad, when all she wanted was to prove to him that she could do the musical. "I have to be there," she told him. "It's a weekend of rehearsals."

"I understand, but still—you say the number and we'll go home."

"You have to come up with a better code word than 'seven.'"

"It was your first racing number! Fine, I could say 'fifty-four.'"

"You could say literally *anything else*."

They shared a small smile. Nat's dad started the engine, and a gust of AC spread the tears around Nat's face. "I don't care if I have to stay with you all night," he said. "Okay?"

"Please don't crash the camping retreat, Dad. That would be so weird."

"I'll blend right in. I'll be the best tree the stage has ever seen."

"Dad!" Nat shook her head and rolled her eyes. She was grateful. Her dad always had her back. He handled every problem with a solution. He never made her feel like a pain or a burden. But she *was* a pain. And a burden.

"Been listening to this great song," he said. "Mind if I put it on?"

Nat shrugged a *Sure*. Up through the speakers came "Dear Theodosia" from *Hamilton*, a ballad sung by Burr about his baby daughter. Nat wanted to acknowledge how sweet it was, but for the first time, the lyrics made her feel like an actual baby, stuck and alone. She thought about how being paralyzed meant her body didn't do what she asked it to do. How gravity sucked. How she had to use her upper-body muscles to carry her entire weight. Like, when she transferred in and out of a car, she felt heavy. Her therapist back in California described disability like that. She'd say, "It's like an added weight you carry around." With Nat's disability, though, the weight was literal. Especially today. Had she gotten on the inaccessible bus and had to rely on someone to lift her in and out, she would have felt stuck on top of her everyday stuckness. She couldn't let that happen.

"Have you spoken to Chloe lately?" her dad asked after a few minutes.

"Um, a little." Actually, they kept missing each other. The time difference was tough. And when they texted or chatted online, something felt off. Like, she could feel their 2,928 miles of separation in Chloe's underuse of the heart emoji.

"Want to give her a ring now?" he asked. "I haven't spoken to the kiddo since the cross-country drive."

"I guess, sure," Nat said, even though she knew it was early morning in California and, with her luck, they'd call Chloe while she was sleeping or in the shower. Or maybe she'd just press ignore.

Her dad used his booming coach voice. "Call Chloe."

"*Calling Chloe,*" the car replied.

Ring, ring. Nat felt her heart skip a little. Earlier that week, she'd wanted to talk to Chloe so badly. To tell her everything that had been going on. Like dancing with Hudson and flirting with Malik and breezily relying on Rey's superhuman arm strength. But now, all she could think about was what had happened today.

Eight rings deep, and Nat was sure they'd missed each other. Again. She went to hang up when Chloe answered, surprisingly bubbly. "Hey!"

"Hey!" Nat said. "What are you— What are you up to?"

"You know, same old— Wait, *chica*, how's your crush?"

Nat's dad shot her a look. She ignored it, keeping focused on a DEER CROSSING sign in the distance.

"I'm on speakerphone, aren't I?" Chloe asked.

"Yup. I'm in the car with my dad, driving up to—"

"What's up, Jeff? How's the new job treating you? Lots of prep before the school year starts?"

Nat watched her dad light up and drum the steering wheel. "Getting a curriculum in order, organizing equipment. But don't worry about me," he said, winking at Nat. "I'll let you two catch up. Just pretend I'm not here."

"Oh, okay," Chloe said, followed by silence.

Four days ago, Nat had left Chloe a voicemail about *like*-liking Malik. She wanted to tell Chloe that she'd spent an hour, maybe three, scrolling through the Archives page of the Broadway Bounders' website in search of his face, even though she saw it in real life every day. She'd wanted to tell her how Hudson thought Malik was cute, too. And even though Malik would probably end up with Savannah, it was still fun to crush on him because they seemed to have an astrological connection and, like, a normal connection, too. They'd shared pretzel sticks! Chloe hadn't called her back.

"Hey, so where have you been—?" Nat started.

"HEY, HERE!" Chloe suddenly shouted back, seemingly not to her.

Nat recognized the sound of waves crashing onto the shore. "Are you at the beach?" she asked. "God, I miss the beach."

"Uh-huh!" Chloe replied. "Fort Point."

"Like, *our spot* at Fort Point?"

"Yeah. So. Many. Surfers." Chloe laughed. "Don't worry, Jeff. We totally *don't* study hot boys as they ride the waves."

"*Okay*," Nat's dad said.

"But it's, like, super early," Nat went on, bulldozing over the awkward. "Chlo, since when are you a morning person?"

Just then, Nat heard a girl's nasal voice say, "Check out this towel. It's bamboo, so the sand doesn't stick." It was familiar, kind of.

"That's so cool," Chloe said.

"Got you a Vitaminwater and a buttered bagel."

"Woo! Thank you! You're my boo."

What was going on? Why was Chloe at the beach, at their sacred spot, at, like, eight AM? And who was this mysterious person bringing her a buttered bagel, when they both knew cream cheese and jelly was her thing?!

"HEY, HOT STUFF!" the nasal voice now screamed.

"OMIGOD, NO!" Chloe squealed. "STOP. I CAN'T!"

Nat couldn't take it. "Who is that?!" she asked.

"H-huh?" Chloe replied, suddenly sounding faraway and out of breath. "Oh, it's Beatrice."

"Chu?"

"Yeah."

"You and Beatrice are at our spot?"

"It's our spot, but it's also a lot of people's spot."

"And you're there crack early because . . . ?"

"TO SHARK!" Beatrice shouted. "It's catcalling but reversed, since we do it to guys."

Nat's dad broke his vow of silence again. "C'mon, girls, that doesn't make it any better."

Beatrice laughed. "Why does Natalie sound like a man?"

"You're on speaker with Jeff," Chloe whispered.

"WHO'S JEFF?" Beatrice asked, extra loud.

"Nat's dad."

"Why are we talking to Natalie's dad?" She laughed some more.

Nat looked over at her dad. He was gripping the steering wheel now, his eyes bulging with discomfort.

"Okay, bye, Natty," Chloe said. "Bye, Jeff. Have fun in the car!"

"Yeah, I'm not just in the car, I'm—" Before Nat could say "headed to a cast retreat," there was a dial tone.

Nat watched the foresty highway turn cliffside as her thoughts smacked into one another. *Beatrice? Really?* Chloe could do better than her. Beatrice called people out when they wore the same outfit twice in two weeks. She told everyone she was a "raw vegan" but then drank cafeteria chocolate milk when her "blood sugar was low." She bragged that she'd gone backstage after *Hamilton* on Broadway three times, even though she'd never posted any pictures backstage or any pictures of New York City in general.

"Chloe was just in the middle of something," Nat's dad said, trying too hard. "I bet you two will talk lots after the retreat."

Sure. Whatever. Chloe's replaced me with Beatrice. She has new friends and so do I. Except my friends ignore me through bus windows.

"How much longer?" Nat grumbled as rolling hills started to pop up on the horizon. They were pimples compared to the epic San Franciscan hills.

"About an hour."

"But we've been driving for, like, an hour and a half."

Nat's dad winced. "I *might* have made an innovative turn. I turned the GPS off since we were following the bus. But then I realized I was following a *different* bus." He sighed apologetically.

"It's fine," Nat said, and she actually meant it. It was probably better to slip into the action than to arrive at the same time as everybody else. She didn't really feel like being around people right now, anyway. She took out the *Wicked* book from her backpack and flipped to page 180, the start of "Part Three: City of Emeralds." She tried to read about Fiyero and Elphaba running into each other three years after graduating from Shiz University, but the words were blending together, not sinking in. *There's no place like home* was all she could think instead. With Chloe as her best friend. With people like the Zoomers, who understood her. With a community who was used to her chair and, for the most part, triple-checked accessibility.

Nat closed the book and, with it, her eyes. Sun specks danced across her eyelids. Her hair thrashed against her face. Moving along the highway with no effort, she felt like Elphaba—*free*. She wished she could drive on forever and never stop for anyone, with no one having to stop for her. She wished gravity would shove it.

CHAPTER ELEVEN

There's a Fine, Fine Line

Nat transferred into Peaches, her palms sweaty from stress. At the moment, the campground's entrance was void of people. If it weren't for the distant singing of "One Short Day" and the hint of orange in the coals of the barbecue stations, she'd swear she was in an abandoned rest stop.

"Want to follow the voices?" her dad asked.

"Um, yeah." Nat stared down at the ground ahead. It was all wood chips, tree roots, and overgrown grass. Oh, and, finally, a hill of San Franciscan proportions.

"I know this retreat is a commitment," Nat's dad said, then slapped a mosquito on his neck. "But I'm going to stay local for an hour in case you end up changing your mind."

Nat took a moment, listening to the lyrics swirl through the trees, when, suddenly, two heads budded up from the top of the hill. Then she saw necks, torsos, and legs, grapevining full steam ahead toward her.

"NAT, YOU'RE HERE!" Rey called, clutching a hot dog in each hand. Hudson was beside her, wearing a circular backpack that was knocking up and down like a loose turtle shell. They were both in neon-green-and-pink tie-dye T-shirts with Oz in iron-on letters. Smattered on the shirts were globs of glitter glue.

"Hey!" Nat said, forcing a smile to match their enthusiasm. "What's been going on?"

Rey looked at Hudson and shrugged. "Spontaneous singing between bites of burger."

"Fig was singing exclusively in goat," Hudson said. "Even though he's playing the Wizard, not Doctor Dillamond—the character who actually morphs into a goat."

Rey laughed. "He was like, 'Bah-bah!' and then Kyle, who is *actually* playing Doctor Dillamond, told him to shut up because he thought Fig was trying to steal his part."

"Kyle sounds like a deranged baby when he baas," Hudson said.

Between the matching outfits and the inside jokes, Nat felt like calling it. She turned around while they shared a laugh, suddenly remembering her dad was still there—*how awkward*—but somehow he'd retreated to the car without her noticing, leaving her overnight bag in the dirt.

"Oh, almost forgot," Rey said, offering Nat a hot dog. "I put mustard on it for you. I hope you like mustard."

"Wow, I do. Thanks," Nat said, then took a delicious bite.

"And one more thing!" Rey untucked a T-shirt from the back of her shorts and tossed it into Nat's lap. "Made you one last night."

"Ahemmm," Hudson said.

"*Hud* made you one," Rey clarified. "I supervised and might have said, 'Good job.' "

Nat held it up, her heart rising in her chest. Her shirt matched theirs, except the glitter glue had dried in a creepy spiral. "Is this supposed to be a spiderweb or . . . ?"

"A tornado," Hudson said.

"Ohhhh! Like the tornado that strikes in *The Wizard of Oz*?"

"Natalie Beacon for the win."

Nat heard a timid *beep* and turned around. There was her dad, waving goodbye and mouthing something like "Wah ow," which was *not embarrassing at all*.

"What's he saying?" Hudson asked.

"No idea." Nat called toward the parking lot, "What, Dad? Can you just *say it*?"

He popped his head out the window. "One hour, Natty. I'll be . . . *around*. Okay?" Then, as if that wasn't strange enough, he winked.

"What's happening in an hour?" Hudson asked.

"Nothing," Nat lied. "I think he wants me to call him if I get service."

Rey pointed at the phone sticking halfway out of Nat's

shorts pocket. "If you have literally any provider, you don't get service here."

And . . . she guessed she was staying.

"I'll show you the girls' cabin," Rey said. "Most people are still eating by the picnic benches, but swimming's next on the agenda. Then we break out into small group rehearsals."

Nat followed Rey around the hill rather than over it, occasionally asking for a push.

"Are you going to swim?" Rey asked Nat as she helped her over the wooden lip of the stairless porch. "Because you totally don't have to. Some people just hang by the sand."

Nat could feel her face tense up. "Yeah, I'll swim. I swim," she said.

"Oh. Cool. Me too."

Inside the cabin, Nat's eyes went to the six bunkbeds lining the perimeter of the room. On each mattress was a sleeping bag, most of them still rolled up, as if the girls had claimed their beds, then made a dash for lunch.

"Take it in," Rey said, whiffing the cabin air. "Do you smell it?"

Nat sniffed. "Wood?"

"MEMORIES! Real ones! Not from *Cats*! Next summer, it'll be stronger for you."

Nat giggled, and Rey slung Nat's bag onto the bottom bunk in the corner closest to the door. On it was a bright yellow sleeping bag. "That's my sister's bag for you. I'm up top. Savannah screamed at me because she didn't want the bunkbed closest to the bathroom, but then I reminded her that girls don't poop or fart, so it's fine."

Nat giggled some more. "Thanks for the sleeping bag. And, honestly, I don't really mind where I sleep."

"Great. 'Cause, apparently, I move A LOT. It's gonna be creaky. Sorry in advance."

Nat transferred onto the bottom bunk and pulled her pillow from her bag. She stared across the room at Savannah's bed, which was made up with real sheets, a comforter, four pillows, and a clip-on fan. Maybe that's why she hadn't joined Nat. Because she'd thought her belongings wouldn't fit in Nat's dad's car.

"Yeah, she really *went for it*," Rey said, following Nat's eyes. She gripped the top of the bunkbed ladder and hung there for a stretch. "By the way, sorry—we had no idea about the bus. If it makes you feel any better, it was mad boring. We didn't even sing all our songs like we did last summer and the summer before. Most of us put in headphones and slept for two hours."

"Thanks," Nat said, half smiling, "for saying that."

Suddenly, they heard a group of girls belting Sia's version of "You're Never Fully Dressed Without a Smile" and stampeding toward the cabin.

"And scene," Rey said, racing into the bathroom with her duffel. "I'm changing before the chaos sets in."

"Okay, good idea," Nat said, already tugging off her shorts. Better now than when everyone would be inside, staring at the science of how she got dressed. She rushed to finish, rolling down her lime-green tankini top as she listened to the girls singing and dancing on the porch. When the song ended, Savannah charged into the cabin, followed by Nicole, Marti, Caitlin, Gia, Sabine, Erica, Leeza, and Jaclyn—all of them buzzing with chatter.

"Hey," Nat said to Savannah, softer than she'd intended.

Oblivious, Savannah climbed up to her bunk. It wasn't until her knees were wobbling over the top ladder rung that she shrieked, "Oh! You're *heeeeere*! I didn't know if you were coming!"

"Why wouldn't she come?" Jaclyn asked from the bed below her.

"Yay! Yay! Yay!" Savannah cheered, clapping her palms against her comforter and producing no sound.

Nat pulled a towel from her bag, slung it over her shoulders, and transferred back into Peaches. "Yeah, anyway," she said, excusing herself. She rolled into the bathroom and waited for Rey to change. It was taking a while, so she backed up against the cubbies, loaded with rough white towels, as girls came in and out to examine themselves in the full-length mirror. Eventually, Savannah came in. She applied lip gloss and made a duck face at herself. Nat stared down at her chipped pink toenails, wishing Rey would hurry up.

It wasn't until everyone had gone that Rey emerged in a ruffled one-piece that looked like it had been fashionable at the turn of the century—and not the most recent one. "Ugh, I hate this," she moaned. "It's my sister's hand-me-down, and it makes me look like a moldy blueberry muffin."

She wasn't wrong. "Well, it's just—"

"You can't tell if it's stained or styled this way on purpose. Whoever designed it should go to jail." Rey tugged the bathing suit over her butt cheeks. "My mom got it from an Indian-owned clothing store, and it's the only suit she'll let us wear. Ironically, it shows *more* of my skin, because my sister's a stick." She released the suit, and it snapped back up her butt crack.

"Honestly, it's fine," Nat said. "It's just us."

"And, like, the whole cast." Rey threw her arms up at the cobwebby ceiling. "Why, God, did you build me like a linebacker?"

"Because you play hard-core sports?"

"I'm throwing shorts on. And a T-shirt. Don't stop me."

Nat followed Rey to her duffel and watched as she hastily tried to get her head through the sleeve of an oversized red *Chicago* T-shirt.

"Everyone has their hang-ups," Nat offered.

Rey emerged from the head hole, and the T-shirt fell to the middle of her thighs. "I know, I know. I'm the worst for complaining." She stepped through a leg of her orange basketball shorts, completing the world's clashiest outfit. "But, seriously, Nat? Look at you. You have the cutest body ever. You're sitting, and you don't even have a pouch of blubber hanging over your bikini bottoms."

Nat looked down at her PacSun suit. It perfectly cupped her B-sized boobs with a sheer divide. The saleswoman had told her it was "hella hot," which was enough of a compliment for Nat to beg her mom to spend forty dollars over the original budget for it.

"You're a ten out of ten in a suit, and you *know it*!"

"I probably wouldn't even qualify for a swimsuit contest," Nat muttered, not wanting to come off as annoyingly body positive when more than half the time she, too, felt like throwing her arms up and griping about how she looked.

"Well, that's messed up," Rey said. "People, pageants—they're dumpster trash."

Nat nodded hard, happy to be in agreement.

Then Rey went quiet and fiddled with a knob on the dresser beside their bunkbed.

"So, should we meet Hudson?" Nat asked, turning her wheels toward the front door.

"I'm really sorry I'm playing Nessa," Rey mumbled.

"What? Why?"

"Savannah told me you'd auditioned for that role, that you really wanted it."

"I did. But that was before I realized Nessarose has to walk in act two." Nat swallowed hard, tumbling into the memory of Savannah breaking the news to her at the audition. "Do you know that the *one song* not on the original Broadway cast recording is 'The Wicked Witch of the East,' where the whole walking thing happens?"

"I know!" Rey said. "It's not one of *Wicked*'s catchier songs."

"Yeah, it's, like, all dialogue."

"But still! How could they have left it off? It's a pivotal moment in the story!"

"No idea. It's unreal!"

"Look, I still feel bad," Rey said. "Your voice is *way* better than mine. Don't say it's not."

Nat sighed, appreciative. "I'm happy where I'm at, as long as Calvin lets me dance."

"Hold up, sister." Rey gripped Nat's shoulders. "I need a sneak peek!"

"HEY, NAT? REY?" a voice called from the porch.

Rey released Nat, and Nat's face got hot. She didn't know if she should run for the door or hide. "Is that M-Malik?"

"I mean, it's just Malik," Rey said. "One 'M.' "

"Ha." Nat's hands were making the decision for her. She was pushing toward the cabin door when it flung open.

Hudson, not Malik, was standing there, wearing white-zinc smudges under his eyes and yellow-ducky swimmies on his arms. "You ready?" he asked nonchalantly.

"Oh, uh. I think." Nat looked around Hudson for Malik, but she was so nervous, all she saw was a blur of green-and-brown trees.

"Let's do this!" Rey said, suddenly beside her in an oversized black-and-white *Phantom of the Opera* T-shirt, which didn't match her orange shorts but certainly clashed less with them.

Hudson held the door as Nat rolled out and Rey followed. Nat's eyes snapped ten feet away to a tetherball court she hadn't noticed until now. Malik was there, punching. As the ball swung around, he caught it with a hair of a delay, about a centimeter from his head. "Wow, I dig your suit green," he said. "I mean, green suit. *Bathing* suit."

"Oh, thanks," Nat replied.

Malik walked toward her in his red swim trunks, which were trendily on the shorter side. He was bare-chested and pretty smooth, except for a few curly wisps of hair.

"LAST ONE TO THE LAKE IS A ROTTEN JAZZ SHOE!" Hudson cried out. He began galloping, dragging Rey by the *Phantom* mask on her shirt.

Rey tried to protest. "Yo! Let's wait for—"

"Nope," he broke in, giving Nat a thumbs-up . . . which he then put in his mouth and sucked as Malik looked at him. *True friendship.*

As Hudson and Rey ran off, Malik speed-walked after them, stumbling over his flip-flops. Meanwhile, Nat pushed beside him, over a tangle of tree roots, trying not to breathe like a monster.

"See that hill?" Malik asked a minute later, his hand protecting his eyes like a visor. "Over it is the lake."

Nat felt a rush of blood go to her head. She could manage the woods, even if it meant going super slow and getting a push here and there, but how was she going to wheel up and over that demon of an incline?!

"Here," Malik said, crouching down with his back to her.

No. He couldn't be serious. "Are you serious?"

"Of course! Hop on!"

"I guess I can, um . . ." Nat's mind began to whirl. *Would she be too heavy? Would he know how to hold her legs? Would too much of her skin be touching too much of his skin? Wait, was she wearing deodorant?!* Tingling with anticipation, she wrapped her arms around his neck. Malik reached behind him, grabbed her legs, and held them around his middle. He stood up like a weight-lifting champion.

"You good?" he asked.

"Yeah," Nat answered, hyperaware of her breath against his neck. Her heart was pounding against his back like a drum solo. Could he hear it? He had to. "Are *you*, um, good?"

"Of course. It's cool to leave your chair back there?"

Peaches? Nope. "Sure, cool."

"Okay, hang on." Malik started jogging. Nat tightened her grip. The sun was scorching, and the humidity was thick.

With every stride, her sticky skin suctioned onto his. They were bumping up and down and down and up, and, somehow, she felt totally secure.

Suddenly, she started to laugh. Malik started to laugh, too. They were two shaken soda cans bubbling, brimming, bursting with joy. He strode through the sand, barely slowing as they met the water. Nat scanned her surroundings. Jaclyn was doing the back crawl to Nicole. Hudson was chilling in the lake, his upper body supported by his swimmies. His feet were resting on Rey's barely submerged shoulders as she tried to stay standing. Fig was mid-cannonball. He made a huge splash, soaking Savannah, who was sunbathing on a floating dock. She shrieked bloody murder as she sat up, propelling cucumber slices from her eyes.

"In or out?" Malik asked Nat, slowing as the water reached his knees.

"IN!"

Malik ran the rest of the way into the water—which was somewhere between freezing and refreshing—until both of their legs were fully under. He flopped forward, and Nat leapfrogged over his head. For a few slo-mo seconds underwater, the two of them were face-to-face, separated only by the bubbles produced by their happy screams.

"Omigod, Malik!" she cried, which sounded like "Omagahmalee!"

"Wahnahwoh!" Malik cried back, which was probably "Whoa, Nat! Whoa!"

Nat could have stayed there forever. No wheelchair, no gravity, and nowhere she couldn't get to by herself. She felt like a mermaid! Except one that relied on, you know, *oxygen*. She swam to the surface, laughing hysterically. He popped up beside her, panting. "Guess you don't need me, huh?"

"*Need you?*" Nat teased, breaking into a front crawl toward Hudson and Rey.

Malik dog-paddled after her. "Dang, you're a good swimmer!" he called, flailing.

"You too," she joked, then swam back to meet him. She noticed his dreads had darkened and expanded in the water, and he had a glint in his eye. It was a glint of panic, but, still, it was striking. "Seriously, you're okay?" she asked.

"I'm just learning," he explained, laughing. "But you—you're a pro!"

Nat used one hand to tread and the other to peel away the heavy curls plastered to the side of her face. "Surprised I can swim?" she asked.

"Nah," Malik said with a shrug, which momentarily sunk him. He bobbed up to chin level, spitting water from his mouth. "You've officially stopped surprising me. Now I just expect you've figured everything out in that creative, Natty way."

"Hey, hang on," she said with a beaming smile. "Let's get you one of Hud's swimmies." They swam together in slippery, clunky unison.

At last, resting on a ducky, Malik grinned with relief. He still had that glint in his eye, but Nat wondered if it was for a whole other reason.

CHAPTER TWELVE

If It's True

"TRUTH!" Fig declared from across the campfire.

"Great," Hudson said. "Because this is a game of Truth or Truth, so truth is literally your only—"

"TRUTH," Fig repeated.

"Jeez. Okay. I'll think of a question."

While Hudson stared into the fire, thinking, Nat snuck a peek at Malik, who was sitting on the log beside her. Against the night sky, his warm eyes shone like two mini moons. Lots of the cast had hung around the firepits after dinner, but it had been a long day of character-building, harmony boot camp, and dialogue speed-throughs, and so, little by little, almost everyone had peeled off to their respective cabins. It was no surprise to Nat that the Oz Bounderz had remained, promising Cora they'd abide by the 10:30 PM curfew.

Nat snuck another glance at Malik. Did he like her or like-like her? She couldn't stop asking herself that question. He seemed to go out of his way to be nice to her, to sit next to her, to talk to her. But Malik was nice to everyone. One smile, and he could make *anyone* feel special.

"You cold? You can have my sweatshirt," Malik whispered to Nat, already unzipping it.

Nat had been feeling the heat from the fire press against her cheeks. Now her cheeks were BURNING. "I'm good, I think," she said. "That's really sweet, though."

"Me! Me!" Savannah exclaimed from Malik's other side, eclipsing their moment. Nat tried not to watch Malik place his sweatshirt around Savannah's theatrically shivering shoulders. "It's always so chilly here at night. You can never get enough layers."

Jaclyn took off her army button-down and draped it on top of the sweatshirt around Savannah's shoulders. Everyone cracked up. Savannah, who was clearly loving the attention, flung the shirt back at Jaclyn.

"Okay, Fig, here's—your—question!" Hudson broke in, clapping. "Deep down, are you trying to steal away Kyle's role as Doctor Dillamond?"

Fig answered, deadpan, "Yes, absolutely. As the Wizard, it's within my power to take what I want. And I want to baaaaa onstage." He got on all fours and baaed his heart out, and the group heaved with laughter. "Okay, Hudson's turn," Fig said, snapping back into his human, two-legged self. "Dare?"

Hudson gave him a stare like, *Ha-ha, NOPE.*

"Truth it is." Fig massaged his nonexistent chin hairs. "What's something that drags you down day-to-day?"

"Wow," Savannah said. "Serious much?"

"A serious game for serious actors," he defended, shoving a melty Swedish Fish into his mouth. "Hud, your response?"

Hudson hesitated. "My, uh, family?"

Rey snapped her fingers in solidarity.

"I'm the weird tap dancer in a preppy family of lacrosse players," he explained. "All three of my brothers play on school teams and travel teams. They bring home massive trophies. My parents literally have a showroom. They—"

"Hey, I made you a trophy last summer," Rey cut in. "Did you ever add it?"

"It was a Barbie you spray-painted gold."

"Not the question."

Hudson sighed. "My parents love and support me, but it's always 'Oh, Hudsy, you have such agile feet. Put them to good use, and maybe you'll get a scholarship. Wink wink.' "

"I love how they *say* 'wink wink,' " Rey said with a chuckle. "My mom keeps shoving me toward a career in psychology. It's, like, *hello*, I'm thirteen. Not twenty-nine. I feel like twenty-nine is a good age to become a psychologist."

"Is your mom a psychologist?" Fig asked Rey.

"No, she's a glassblower."

Fig arched an eyebrow. "She blows on glass?"

"She makes glass art."

"For psychologists?"

Rey interlocked her fingers and pushed out her arms. "She says that psychology is the closest job to theater, except it'll make you more money. My parents think I'm a bundle of potential, and they're relying on me to support them when they're old, since my sister is a freelance sculptor for PETA—the animal rights group."

"That's a REAL JOB?!" Jaclyn asked.

"Yuuup." Rey looked at Malik. "Your parents are lawyers, right?"

"Yeah," Malik answered.

"Do they sit around demanding that you pursue lawdom or whatever?"

"Nah. My dad was a theater major, and my mom played drums for a touring band in her twenties, so they're pretty chill."

Rey slapped her thighs. "See? That's what I'm talking about! My parents are artists. My sister is an artist. But with me, they act like the arts are just for fun." She leaned forward with so much passion, she nearly tipped off her log. "I don't even need to act. I can direct! Build sets! Be an Indian-accent consultant! Whatever!" She jumped up and shouted, "I'll literally do ANYTHING to stay part of THE THEATER!"

"What about veterinary school?" Hudson asked.

"Oh, yeah. I'd be a vet, too."

Malik raised an arm, freeing it from Savannah's snuggle.

"Okay, I've got a truth," he said. "Real talk: I'm the only Black kid. Not just in this show, but, like, in my school."

"Don't you go to Martin Luther King Jr. Middle School?" Fig asked.

"Yee-up," he said. "It's weird for me when we learn stuff about slavery or the Harlem Renaissance because the white teachers talk directly to me. Like, they're checking to make sure they're delivering the right info or something. Or maybe because they think, 'Oh, Malik's Black. This is *his* history, something he should really absorb.' It's so embarrassing."

Again, Rey snapped in solidarity.

"We're glad you're sharing," Savannah said, putting a hand on his knee.

"Thanks," Malik said. "At least when I act in shows, it doesn't matter. The original Broadway Fiyero wasn't Black. Theater isn't black and white."

"It's gray," Savannah said.

"Sure. It's all the colors. Directors cast you for what you can bring to the role."

Nat glanced at a nodding Hudson, remembering their conversation about how audiences willingly suspend their disbelief when seeing live theater. For Malik, casting directors seemed to trust that idea. But Malik was Malik—charming and talented and mature. OF COURSE no one cared that the color of his skin didn't match the original casting of a character.

"Anyway," Malik said. "Someone else can go."

"I'll share my truth," Jaclyn said, tossing a gum wrapper into the fire. "My hamster, Sally Bowles, died last week, and she's been visiting me in my sleep."

"Like, in your dreams?" Fig asked.

"No, like, I get up to pee, and her ghost is in the toilet."

"What does she say to you?"

"Nothing. She's a hamster. But, like, when my guinea pig, Roxie Hart, died two years ago, she also haunted me and then my a cappella competition got snowed out. A coincidence? I think not."

"I don't think our show is going to get snowed out in summer," Rey said.

"Stranger things have happened. Also, can you ask your sister how much for a sculpture? It's a great alternative to taxidermy."

"Ew," Savannah said.

"Her rates are on her website," Rey responded. "I'll DM you."

"Moving on, that was frightening," Fig said. "Who's next? Savannah? Nat?"

Savannah looked up at the stars, seemingly in deep concentration.

"You can go if you want," Nat offered, her heart suddenly pounding with anticipation. She had no idea what she'd say. She mentally replayed everyone else's responses for inspiration. Instead, a sinking realization hit. She'd been quiet the whole time.

"My sister has issues," Savannah uttered, then looked directly at Nat. "Next!"

"What . . . issues?" Nat asked.

"My turn's over, go," Savannah said.

"Okay." Embarrassed for prying, Nat's mind went extra blank. She felt like she was having one of those actor nightmares, where you forget your lines in the middle of a performance. "Can someone ask me a question?" she blurted. "Ask me anything, really."

The stars dulled as a hazy cloud set in. Then there were crickets. Literal ones. After what felt like a full minute, Rey carefully spoke up. "We actually don't know why you're in a wheelchair . . ."

Nat looked down at her chair. She hadn't realized she'd never told her friends about what had happened. Everyone at home, even people she wasn't that close to, they just knew.

"Sorry, I'm a jerk," Rey said quickly. "You seriously don't have to talk about it—"

"I'll tell you guys," Nat said. "I honestly didn't mean to keep it a secret."

"Are you *sure*?"

Nat nodded, and her heart got heavy and bouncy all at once. She took a deep breath and focused on Rey as she began. "When I was two years old, I was in a car accident. My parents and I were on the highway, and a guy driving in the opposite direction was distracted, on his phone. He flipped over the divider, and his car came down on ours pretty hard. The guy survived, everyone did, and I became paralyzed. I have a spinal cord injury, which means that the messages my brain sends to my body through my spinal cord don't get through. I basically learned to wheel right after I learned to walk."

Nat broke her focus from Rey to glance around the campfire. She expected her friends to be acting uncomfortable and pitying—staring sadly at the flickering flames or, like, frowning at her—but everyone was giving her their attention, listening with open hearts. Even Savannah.

"Wow," Fig said after a few seconds.

"Yeah, wow," Hudson repeated.

"Thanks for telling us," Rey said. "That was probably hard. Was it hard?!"

"No, not really." Nat rode a wave of relief as a few refreshing raindrops sprinkled down from the sky. "Normally, racing kids ask me outright, in a competitive way, to see who's been in a chair for longer. Or no one asks at all. At least to my face."

"I guess we should have asked sooner," Malik said. "Our bad."

"I swear it's fine," Nat said. "It was good to get to know you all without having to explain my whole backstory first. Anyway, the accident was a long time ago, and I don't really remember it. I mean, I don't like talking about it in front of my parents, because they *do* remember it, and it was really traumatic for them to see me go through everything, but telling my story reminds me of what I've been through. People look at me—whether they're friends or just random people on the street—and I know they wonder."

"Is it hard being in a chair?" Jaclyn asked.

"No, it's normal to me," Nat replied. "It's all I know, so it's not like I miss being able to walk or feel my legs." She glanced at Malik, desperate to know how all this was hitting him. He had his elbows on his knees and was soaking it all in. Satisfied, she went on. "Also, I think because it happened when I was young, I developed with my spinal cord injury. I was learning how to dress myself the same time you all were, just in my own way."

"So, since the accident happened a long time ago," Hudson said, "it's not like you're dealing with the shock of it, right?"

"Right."

"And so being in a car is fine for you?"

"Exactly. Actually, I love driving in a car, since it's one of the only ways I can be in motion without my chair. Plus, anyone looking at me through the window might think I'm just a normal thirteen-year-old. It's kind of freeing."

Hudson smirked. "Literally no one has ever looked at me and thought, 'Oh, a *normal* kid.' "

"I can't relate," Fig joked, twirling an especially bright purple curl in his fingers. "Everyone assumes I'm entirely normal at all times."

As Nat giggled, the wind started to howl. The humidity hugged her tight. She had no idea how Savannah was wearing Malik's sweatshirt without sweating.

"So, I'm confused," Savannah said. "Why wouldn't you come on the bus?"

Rey delivered Savannah a death stare.

"Well, I guess . . ." Nat paused, urging herself to be polite. "A car I can transfer in and out of by myself. A bus, though? Not so much."

Everyone nodded, probably glad Nat had an easy answer. The continued support made her feel warm and fuzzy. It didn't hurt that Malik had chosen that moment to slip his hand inside hers. "Some people wonder if I was born this way because of a disease or something at birth. I actually have a lot of friends who have disabilities because of—"

"Enough dark stuff!" Savannah broke in. "Come on, guys. This is supposed to be fun!"

"It *is* fun," Malik said, letting go of Nat's hand. "Learning about each other is cool."

"Sure," she said. "But you know what's *cooler*? Stealing s'mores supplies! They store them in the ranger station. I saw the rangers return them there after dinner."

"That *does* sound cool. See you in a bit!" Hudson said, waving her goodbye. Savannah scoffed, and he turned his attention back to Nat. "I knew that whatever happened, it had to have been a while ago based on how kick-butt you are at . . . DANCING!" He air-high-fived her from across the campfire. "That's right. Nat and I have been hard at work on our own choreo, and it's going to be AMAZEBALLS!"

Nat blushed, the heat of her skin fighting against the heat of the flames.

"You have to show us!" Rey exclaimed. "Dance! Do it!"

Nat and Hudson exchanged a *Should we?!* look, when, suddenly, the rain sprinkles turned into drops the size of piano keys. The fire started to stretch and thin, and Nat had to peel her already soaked hair from her cheeks.

"DANCE IN THE RAIN!" Fig shouted.

"SING IN THE RAIN!" Jaclyn shouted.

Nat appreciated the enthusiasm, but dancing on the dirt would have been hard enough. Muddy puddles? Impossible.

"*DANCE, DANCE, DANCE!*" Rey, Fig, Jac, and Malik chanted, while Savannah shrank inside Malik's hood, pulling the drawstring tight under her chin.

"I just— I can't," Nat gurgled as the rain smacked her lips.

"This diva needs her *stage*!" Hudson called out. "These conditions are not up to union standards."

The chanting persisted until the first lightning cracked. The sky lit up in Harry Potter–scar zigzags. Savannah thrust herself from the log, screaming. Everyone else shot up and stared at one another like, *Are we making a run for it?* And then, just as the thunder rumbled, the Oz Bounderz started sprinting, boys and girls in opposite directions toward their cabins. Nat channeled her inner racer girl and wheeled ahead, her tires bulldozing down the path.

"Ah! Gross! Wet!" Savannah squealed as she came up splashing beside Nat. "Do you need help?"

Nat glanced behind her, wondering if she was only offering to impress Malik. But Malik was halfway up the hill behind them, way too far to hear. "I'm okay," she said. "Just might need a push where the tree roots are like witch fingers."

"Okay!" Savannah slowed down, her sandals sinking into the mud. Out of politeness, Nat relaxed her grip on the wheels to match her pace. "Malik is soooo nice to you," Savannah purred. "It's actually really inspiring. I mean, he carried you all the way to the lake!"

"Well, yeah . . ."

"I feel like he helps you when I'm around in order to, like, impress me. But whatever, it's working! He's honestly, like, the most gentlemanly, mature guy."

Nat wasn't stupid—she could see what Savannah was doing. And it was making her heart drop.

"We should do something nice for him in return, don't you think?"

Nat was afraid to ask. "What do you mean?"

"Boys are oblivious. Somehow, he has no idea I like him. And Calvin cut all the stage kisses to make the show more 'family friendly,' so it's not even like I can rely on the sparks flying when our lips touch."

Thank God.

"Anyway, you two seem close. Like, I notice he really listens to you. Can you talk to him for me?"

Nat plowed through a giant puddle, trying to wrap her head around what Savannah was saying. Savannah believed Malik had carried Nat to the pool—that he'd held her hand—to show off to Savannah, not because he had a crush on Nat. Savannah wasn't trying to make Nat feel small so she'd back off from Malik. She didn't see Nat as a threat at all. She saw her only as the perfect wingwoman.

The lightning cracked harder, and a tree snapped in the distance. Nat didn't even flinch. What if Savannah was right? What if Malik didn't have a crush on Nat but was just being a good friend to her? If Malik learned about Savannah's crush, then of course he'd ask her out. She was super pretty and super confident and super talented, to boot. She had to be everything Malik would want in a crush. *Ugh, nooooooooooooo.*

"SO, WILL YOU TALK TO MALIK FOR ME?" Savannah shouted over a roar of thunder. "I THINK WE BOTH AGREE HE DESERVES SOMEONE AMAZING."

CHAPTER THIRTEEN

I'm Here

"FIVE, SIX, SEVEN, EIGHT," Calvin called out during their gazillionth run-through of "Dancing Through Life." On the moves that were supposed to pop, he extended his arms so fast and intensely, they looked like they would burst out of their sockets. "BAH-PAH!"

From her boring, still corner, Nat could see that it was challenging for her castmates to move freely onstage with half a dozen scattered buckets collecting raindrop leakage from the storm. The rain hadn't let up since the retreat, and Saddle Stream's streets had never been so flooded. Nat's dad couldn't believe rehearsal hadn't been canceled. He'd actually tried to convince Nat to skip it, but he didn't understand the whirling world of theater, even weeks away from opening night.

He also didn't know about today's plan: Nat would prove to Calvin that she was capable of dancing in the group numbers just like the rest of the ensemble. It was the first rehearsal following the retreat, and Calvin had asked Nat to stay for the full day of choreography since they were drilling the musical numbers—the singing, acting, and dancing all together. Hudson was confident she was ready. Nat would have liked a few more days of rehearsal. She really couldn't blow this.

"FOCUS!" Calvin shouted. "Remember, everyone has different circles of concentration, but one of them must be our star couple! In other words, EYES ON MALIK AND SAVANNAH!"

Nat stayed stationed in the corner, listening to the downpour slam against the windows and watching Malik's hand move to the small of Savannah's back. They were swaying and dipping, giggling and flirting, and, every once in a while, Savannah would snap her head to Nat for a quick girl-gossip smile that said, *You see? We're perfect together.*

Nat felt dizzy. *Savannah might not be acting her feelings, but Malik is,* she tried to tell herself. *He's in character. Or at least I hope he is.* Ugh. She gladly shifted her eyes from Malik to the clock at the back of the theater. 2:07 PM. How had they only been rehearsing for four hours?!

During what had felt like twenty torturous hours, Nat had flip-flopped between feeling bored watching *everyone else* in the ensemble dance and anxious over finding the right time to face Calvin. She and Hudson had psyched themselves up to confront him first thing in the morning—they'd rip it off like a Band-Aid! But Nat had said, "Excuse me?

Calvin?" and he'd looked over her and shouted at the kids in the audience, "A LITTLE RAINFALL, AND HALF OF YOU HAVE ARRIVED FIVE MINUTES LATE?!" So, Nat and Hudson had gotten out of the way.

They'd later tried to approach Calvin at the start of the midmorning break, but before either of them could get a word in, he and Cora had scrambled past them for a Starbucks run. They'd returned to the lobby ten minutes later, totally wet and reeking of cigarette smoke, and when Hudson went to say something to Calvin then, Calvin had barged past him into the theater, clapping the cast to attention and shouting, "TAKE IT FROM THE TOP OF 'MARCH OF THE WITCH HUNTERS' BEFORE I LOSE MY WITCHING MIND!!!"

Nat might have lost her witching mind, too. Now she watched Malik and Savannah perform a lift—a move that Calvin had choreographed but that Hudson had shaped to mimic the famous lift in *Dirty Dancing.* Savannah ran and jumped up, and as Malik slowly spun her around, his arms shaking, Savannah's knees buckled. Her legs dropped down a second later, almost nailing Malik in the privates. She shrieked. He grunted. Nat wished she didn't have to watch them practice anymore. She wished she didn't have to pretend to be infatuated with them as a pair.

"NAT, YOU'RE—NOT—IN THIS—PART," Calvin barked on beat. "EXIT! EXIT STAGE RIGHT."

Her face burning with embarrassment, Nat began to wheel offstage. She put her head down as she passed Malik, but then she spotted black Sharpied words on his silver Nike high-tops—DANCE THRU LIFE—and she stopped dead in her tracks.

"Are you thinking of running me over again?" he cracked.

Nat involuntarily laughed. She looked up at him. He smiled, his baby-blue-braced teeth popping. Her heart began railing against her chest. *I can do this. I have to do this.*

"OFF!" Calvin barked at her.

Nat shot Hudson a look. *I'm doing this.*

He widened his eyes like, *Now? Are you serious?!*

She nodded. *Wish me luck.* She rolled downstage past Rey and Kyra and faced Calvin, whose attention had already shifted to the dancing ensemble. With all the courage she could muster, she began, "Actually, I was thinking—"

"BAH-PAH!" Calvin shouted, popping his curled fingers from loose fists. "*Dancing through liiiiiife.* Avi, turn downstage."

Try again, louder. "I can dance if you'll give me a chance!" She hadn't meant to rhyme like that. "I mean, I can dance if you'll give me the *opportunity*."

The music was accelerating. In her peripheral vision, she could see Molly, Amy, and Erica dancing on— right hand up, left hand up, leap, arabesque, turn. Confused, Cora opened her mouth to respond to Nat, but Calvin barked again, silencing her. "AVI, THE *OTHER* DOWNSTAGE."

Nat piped up, maybe too loudly. "I CAN DANCE LIKE EVERYONE ELSE!!"

Cora tried to whisper in Calvin's ear. He held up his hand, sending her stumbling backward. Instead, he addressed Hudson. "*HELLO*, EARTH TO BOQ! THAT'S YOUR CUE!"

Hudson obeyed and started prancing toward Rey. He accidentally jazz-kicked a bucket three feet across the stage, sending water sloshing over the edge. "Sorry!"

"Watch it! Sabine, you're closest to the mop. Hudson, carry on!"

Hudson froze. "I know, but did you hear Nat?" Calvin shoved his arms out, like, *Go already, we're in the middle of the number!* But Hudson tucked his thumbs into the elastic of his gym shorts, nervously demanding Calvin's attention.

"Where's your head, Hud?" Calvin snapped.

Hudson pointed to his head. "Nat and I want to show you something."

Nat should have stayed focused on Calvin. That would have made her look strong. But by now, only a third of the cast was still dancing, and she needed to know if Malik was one of them. She craned her neck and saw Savannah swipe for Malik's hand as it hung by his side. He'd stopped dancing! He was watching her encouragingly. Relieved and nervous all at once, Nat twisted back toward Calvin.

Their eyes locked, and it was . . . scary.

"You know what?" he said, spit spraying from his mouth. "Lulu, stop the music."

With an exasperated sigh, Lulu lifted her fingers from the keys. The final chord rang out and then faded, cuing the entire cast to stop dancing. The silence chilled the theater.

"You want to dance, Nat?" Calvin asked. "Show me."

Nat felt her ears go red.

"We don't have a lot of time," Calvin pressed. "C'mon."

"Can you play the music, Lulu?" Hudson asked. "From the top of the dance break?"

"Sure thing." Lulu flipped back through the score and then, with absolutely no warning, started playing.

"You ready?" Hudson whispered to Nat. She had no idea. She had no choice. Calvin was impatiently glaring with his arms crossed, and the music was only eight counts away from the combination that she and Hudson had been practicing for weeks. She faced upstage.

"And a five, six, seven, eight!" Hudson called out to her.

Nat popped a wheelie and rocked back and forth. She landed a half turn with purpose, took a big roll downstage, then threw her hands up in the air. She clapped over her head and then gracefully spiraled her hands down to her lap. *Slap!* She rolled to the left, then rolled to the right. The stage lights weren't on, but she swore she felt blinded. She kept dancing, getting deeper in character. She wasn't onstage at the JCC. She wasn't at the cheesy dance at Shiz University, either. She was at the Ozdust Ballroom—the most swankified place in town!

Hudson joined her, and they moved in sync. He held her hand tight as she threw her body weight to her right side and pulled her left wheel up. She balanced on one big wheel for two counts before she came back down. She slapped her knees and then stretched her arms out to her sides. She went on like this for a minute, growing more and more confident, then geared up for the big turn with a fast breath. *Booyah!* She nailed the 360 in a wheelie! *And . . . Finished!*

Panting, she smiled out at the audience. She expected applause, nods, smiles, cheering, chanting—all the enthusiasm!—but only Cora was giving her positive vibes. Lulu was eyeing Calvin subordinately, and Calvin was fanning himself with his *Newsies* cap. "That was . . ." he began.

That was WHAT?! Nat was sure there was something negative coming. *That was fine, but it's not the same choreography. We don't have time to add you into the group numbers. Isn't your dancing going to be distracting?*

Instead Calvin said, "Nat, that was FANTASTIC."

Fantastic, fantastic, fantastic. Nat heaved a euphoric sigh.

Calvin fluttered his lips apologetically. "I didn't mean to be so abrasive. Those who've done the show with me before can speak to my *intensity*." There were a few affirming mumbles and giggles. He pressed his lips together and nodded at Hudson and then again at Nat. "Nice job, you two."

Nat's heart shot up, practically through her vocal cords. "So, that means what?"

"Cora marks all the blocking and choreography in her big book, so if it's all right with her—"

"It's all right with me," Cora cut in with waving *YAY!* arms.

"Then dance away, Nat," Calvin said. "You're welcome to participate in any of the group numbers you'd like."

"I'd like to do them all!" Nat blurted out.

"Well, I should warn you I don't have a lot of time to incorporate you into the dances."

"On it," Hudson assured him, clutching his shorts with tight fists. "We'll work on translating and blocking and will make it work with what you've got, I promise."

"Yup, on it for sure," Nat chimed in.

"I don't normally like surprises," Calvin mused. "But this was a delightful surprise."

Nat sat in the sweet thickness of his compliment, beaming. Hudson put his hand over her hand, which was still anxiously gripping her wheel. He squeezed. She let go of her wheel, and some of her anxiety, and squeezed back.

"Hey, Calvin," Cora said, clicking on the stopwatch around her neck. "Hate to halt the love fest, but it's time for a five-minute break. We good?"

"Yeah," Calvin said, unusually friendly. "Okay, everyone, take five! Refuel!"

"*THANK YOU, FIVE!*" everyone in the room chanted back.

As Calvin practically bounced up the aisle, Nat's excitement bubbled in her chest. Once the doors slammed behind him, all that excitement exploded out of her mouth and arms. "AHHHHHH! WHAT?! HOW DID– OMIGOD, OMIGOD, OMI-G-O-D!" she screamed over Hudson's "GAHWAHWOWAHHHHHH!" They slapped hands on repeat and squealed. Hudson jumped up and down, his fingers locked in Nat's, and her arms flung up and down with him.

"Aw, you guys are so happy," Savannah said, skipping over to them. "Nat, your little dance is adorable."

Nat would never define what she'd just done as "little" or "adorable." Hard-core, athletic, groundbreaking, maybe.

Savannah whispered into Nat's ear, "Did you talk to Malik about me yet?"

Before Nat could shake her head, she felt big, warm, citrus-smelling hands over her eyes.

"Guess who?"

"Malik."

"Hey, how'd you know?"

Your tangy smell. Your smooth voice. "No idea."

Malik laughed and popped around to face her. "Yo, so that was amazing! You CRUSHED IT!" Then he hugged her.

Nat could feel herself radiating. "Thanks," she said.

"Malik, are you ready to practice now?" Savannah asked. Her pink ballet flats were suddenly shoving between Nat's chucks and Malik's high-tops. "We really have to work on our lift." Before he could answer, she was backing up and then racing into his arms. Nat watched Malik hold Savannah up, the outline of his arm muscles popping, but then the lights began to flicker and the two of them crashed to the floor.

"OWWWW! MALIK!" Savannah cried out.

Nat looked around. Petey, Caitlin, and Jayden gripped one another's arms, frozen with confusion. Erica, Kyra, and Gia stared up at the flickering lights, mesmerized. Rey and Jaclyn stumbled on from backstage, looking around nervously.

"Um, what's happening?" Hudson asked.

"Is it a ghost?" Savannah asked from the floor, curling into Malik. "I'm scared of ghosts."

"It's Sally Bowles, my dead hamster," Jaclyn said.

"Shut up, Jac, this is seeeerious," Savannah whined.

"Oh, I'm serious," Jaclyn said. "I knew Calvin should have done *Cabaret.*"

The flickering suddenly stopped. The lights went out. For a split second, the torrential downpour was the only sound they could hear. Until the screams drowned it out.

"HEY, HEY, EVERYBODY, STAY CALM," Cora commanded, shining a flashlight onto the stage. "IT'S JUST A BLACKOUT!"

Lulu was beside her, shining her iPhone's flashlight.

The cast darted around and into one another, shoving toward backstage, the edge of the stage, wherever they could exit. It was chaos.

"CAN EVERYONE STOP MOVING?" Lulu shouted.

"CORA, WHAT IS GOING ON?!" Calvin shouted from the back of the theater.

"LISTEN TO ME, EVERYONE! CHILL!!!" Cora shouted.

No one listened. The cast's screaming went on in short, frequent bursts. Nat clung to Hudson and he to her, and then Rey's hand was patting Nat's face, completing the clinging triangle.

Madden emerged from backstage, swinging glow tape. "I'VE GOT A SOLUTION!" he shouted, even though the tape didn't illuminate anything except his face. He looked super creepy.

"MADDEN IS SALLY BOWLES, THE HAMSTER GHOST!" Savannah screamed.

And then the fire alarm rang.

"We need to get to the elevator," Rey said, leading the way. She, Hudson, and Nat weaved backstage through scrambling bodies until they arrived at the edge of the ramp. Nat flew down. In the house, they plowed up the aisle, dimly lit by the EXIT sign, then charged through the theater doors. The lobby was almost as dark as the stage. They followed the cast's pounding footsteps toward the elevator, then waited in a massive clump as stacks of fingers hit the down button, pressing and pressing and pressing. The button wasn't lighting up. Neither were the floors.

"Oh, freak, I think it's out," Jaclyn mumbled beside them.

"YO, PAY ATTENTION, ALL," Fig announced. "WE'RE GOING TO HAVE TO TAKE THE STAIRS!"

The stairs?! They were four flights up. Without the elevator, Nat was totally stuck.

Her heart started to pound so hard it seemed to jam up her throat. Or maybe that was the smoke billowing in from the Broadway Bounders office at the end of the hall. Nat squinted at the office through stinging eyes, and, all of a sudden, there was a *crackle crack!* Through the window in the door, there were licking orange flames.

The screaming escalated.

"I got you," Rey said, shoving her back in front of Nat's body. "Hud, take her chair." Nat threw her arms around Rey's neck. Rey held her legs. "Let's go, let's go," Rey muttered, racing toward the stairs. Up and down and up and down they went as a stampede of panicked tweens trailed them, passed them, knocked into them.

Fig was crawling down beside them, headfirst, getting stomped on.

"WHAT ARE YOU DOING?" Hudson yelled at him. "GET UP!"

"NO!" Fig cried. "SMOKE RISES!"

Avi was behind them, rolling down with a thud.

"AND WHAT ABOUT YOU?" Hudson asked him. "AT LEAST CRAWL!"

"Stop, drop, and roll, man."

"JUST RUN, IDIOT!" Hudson screamed. "YOU'RE NOT ON FIRE!"

The fire alarm was ringing so loud Nat couldn't hear herself think. She closed her eyes, coughing into Rey's back. Her brain went black. Then, the next thing she knew, she and Rey were melting into the grass outside the JCC parking lot. Two witches at rock bottom.

Good morning, Broadway Bounders families,

It is with our deepest regret that we are emailing you this morning to inform you that our production of *Wicked* is being pushed back indefinitely. The theater facilities at the Saddle Stream JCC have sustained a lot of smoke damage—in attempt to put out the fire, there was hosing down, which led to flooding, and now everywhere is prone to mold. The JCC has officially shut down their building while they fully assess the damage and then, eventually, begin reconstruction.

We are sad to say that Broadway Bounders has lost our office, offline archives, sets, props, and costumes from the last decade. Because of this, we no longer have the resources, funds, or time this late in the game to book alternate production space. We are grateful, however, that no one sustained any injuries and that everyone is safe.

Cast, you have worked incredibly hard these last several weeks. We are very proud of you. Chins up! Remember, *No one mourns the Wicked*.

For Good,
Calvin, Cora, and Lulu

CHAPTER FOURTEEN

The Smell of Rebellion

Nat stared at the Oz Bounderz chat on her laptop. Her brain was frozen with despair. So were her fingers. She didn't feel like typing. She didn't know what to say.

DearEvanHudson: Noooooooooooooooooooooooo
TheReyWhereItHappens: 😫
LegallySavannah: ummm, is this even legal?!
PurpleHairyPoppins: That's so Glinda of u
LegallySavannah: Thnx, but now I'll never play Glinda
TheSoundOfMalik: I'm just glad we're all alive.
PurpleHairyPoppins: That's so Fiyero of u
JACLYNandHYDE: Anyone else feel like they swallowed their grandpa's cigar?
JACLYNandHYDE: It's like the smoke is lounging in my chest
PurpleHairyPoppins: That's so Elphaba of u

JACLYNandHYDE: I will melt you, you are so annoying
PurpleHairyPoppins: hahahahaha

Nat closed her eyes, and when she opened them, she was staring at the emailed cast list pinned to her wall. A fresh wave of anger rolled through her. She had been so close to not just *being* in a show but DANCING in one. For the first time in her life, she'd proven she was born to be onstage. How could she just let that go?

She looked back at the chat, and a second wave of anger rolled into her fingers. Before she knew it, she was typing.

NatThrowinAwayMyShot: The fire was soooo terrifying.
TheReyWhereItHappens: ch'yuuup
NatThrowinAwayMyShot: We survived for a reason
LegallySavannah: Because we are 2 talented to die
NatThrowinAwayMyShot: Kind of! We can't give up now!
LegallySavannah: I'm sorry, what are you proposing?!
NatThrowinAwayMyShot: That we find a way to do the show!
LegallySavannah: I refuse to do a backyard production
DearEvanHudson: You have a résumé to build
LegallySavannah: Exactly
TheReyWhereItHappens: 😂

Nat couldn't believe her friends were STILL joking around. She'd wanted to be a part of *Wicked*, and so she'd turned her parents' no into a yes. Didn't her friends get it? They didn't have to accept defeat after ONE email!

NatThrowinAwayMyShot: Seriously, though! This can't be the last of the show. Rey didn't carry me down 4 flights of stairs for nothing.

TheReyWhereItHappens: Correct, it was to get my high-intensity workout in.

NatThrowinAwayMyShot: i'll rephrase: we didn't SURVIVE THE FIERY FLAMES FOR NOTHING

LegallySavannah: Dramatic much?

TheSoundOfMalik: Nat, I'm listening.

Nat needed to see her friends face-to-face. She needed to convince them that they could reboot the show. She typed, "Today. 2 pm. My house. Who's in?"

"*Eleka nahmen nahmen*," Fig chanted, sitting with his legs in a pretzel on the floor of Nat's living room. He'd been trying to start a *Wicked*-themed prayer circle for five minutes, and Nat wasn't having the silliness. She'd hoped her friends had agreed to come over because they, too, felt desperate to *do something* to keep the *Wicked* production alive, but, apparently, they just wanted an air-conditioned, unsupervised place to hang out. Fig chanted on. "*Ah tum ah tum eleka nahmen*."

"That's nice, Fig," Nat said, "but prayers aren't going to help us."

"Prayers could help," Savannah countered.

"Okay, say a prayer in your own religion on the count of three," Rey instructed the group. "One, two—"

"I'm an atheist," Fig declared. "Theater is my temple."

"I think we need to do something more *active*," Nat said.

Rey whipped out her workout log from her backpack. "I'm all ears. And muscles."

"I invited you all here because we cannot let a fire stop us." She was met with six stony stares. "Look: We are smart! We are talented! We are ambitious! If we put our heads together, we will find a way to save the show!" She rolled in front of the couch and threw her fist in the air. "*Wicked* for life, or, at least for this summer! Who's with me?"

No fists rose. Hudson looked like he was about to raise his hand, but then he just reached for an oatmeal cookie.

"I'm too traumatized," Savannah whined, making her teeth chatter against her thermos of iced tea. "I can't deal with another rejection if we try and fail."

"We're not going to fail!" Nat argued. "As long as we get everyone on board—"

"We don't have anyone on board," Malik mumbled.

"What do you mean?"

"I texted Calvin to ask if he'd reconsider directing us, and he wrote, 'Go swimming, go hiking, have a summer.' So I texted Lulu, asking if she'd keep musical directing. She said don't text her, so I emailed her. She didn't email me back. Finally, I texted Cora, thinking she'd be down to help us, but her response was no better."

Nat chewed her lip, afraid to ask. "No better how?"

Malik read from his phone. " 'Hi, lovelies. Putting on a show is harder than you think. Do yourselves a favor and hang tight till next summer. I'll help then, I promise!' "

"Yikes," Hudson said, licking cookie crumbs from his fingers. "Without a director, a musical director, or a stage manager, do we really stand a chance?"

"Well . . ." Nat half shrugged, her head spinning for an answer. "Maybe we don't need adult help. We have twenty-four kids in the cast."

"Eighteen," Fig corrected. "Erica, Madden, Sabine, Caitlin, Molly, and Amy quit. Their parents have already transferred them into classes at the Y."

"It's, like, who are we to reboot the show, anyway?" Hudson asked. "We're just a bunch of musical theater dork misfits—"

"Aw, I've never been called a misfit!" Savannah broke in.

"—without any help or money and with, like, six of our castmates out." He groaned at Nat. "I love you, but let's be really real."

Nat felt twelve blazing eyes on her. She wished she'd known all this BEFORE she'd tried to rally everyone. "Fine, you're—" An incoming call from her mom rang out through the landline. "Hold on."

She picked up. "Hi, Mom." Nat let her know that yes, everyone was here, and yes, she'd offered them cookies, and yes, their plan to resurrect the show was still on, sort of, maybe.

And then, about to hang up, Nat's mom said, "Hon, you know, I have an idea for you." *An idea*. Surprised her mom had given any thought to the show, Nat was eager to hear. "We have a nice deck and folding chairs, if you and your friends want to perform for your dad and me later tonight," she offered.

"Maybe," Nat said, because screaming would have made everyone's heads turn.

"I love you."

"Love you, too."

Nat hung up, and Fig was standing on her couch, raising a glass of almond milk and speaking like an old man. "As your great and powerful Wizard, I stand before you to reveal the truth: Oz was very flammable, and my greatness could not stop it from burning to the ground." He chugged the milk and burped. "Let us join hands and pray. *Eleka nahmen nahmen*—"

Jaclyn smacked Fig with a pillow, and he tumbled off the couch, laughing hysterically. Everyone was laughing, except Nat—her mind was blowing up like a string of Christmas lights. Red. Pink. Blue. Green. Orange. Idea. Idea. Idea.

She grabbed her laptop from the coffee table, opened Google Docs, and set up a chart. She labeled it: LET'S GET WICKED. The first row: PERFORMANCE SPACES. The second row: ROLES. The third row: SOCIAL MEDIA. Then she tried to fill in the first set of boxes with whatever she knew about Saddle Stream . . . which wasn't much.

"Nat, uh, what are you doing?" Hudson asked.

She looked up from her screen so fast, she saw staticky pins. "I'm brainstorming ways to get our show back on track."

He felt her forehead. "Did you forget everything we just talked about? *Wicked* is dead."

"No," she said.

"What do you mean, 'No'?"

"I mean . . ." Nat set her laptop at half-mast and looked at Fig. "In *The Wizard of Oz,* Dorothy, Scarecrow, the Tin Man, and the Cowardly Lion travel all this way just to meet the Wizard, as if he can give them what they need. But what happens?"

"The curtain is pulled back on the Wizard," Fig answered.

"Right. The Wizard is a hack. He's just a weak dude speaking into a microphone, and he can't help them. But everything Dorothy and her friends needed was inside them all along."

"So . . . what are you saying?" Rey asked.

"We were about to give up on ourselves because grown-ups like Calvin, Lulu, and Cora told us to. But what do they know? Are we really going to back down before we've even given the show a shot?" Nat looked at her friends, and her mind flashed to her parents and how, with only the best intentions, they'd tried to hold her back. If she'd listened to them, she wouldn't be with these kids right now. She wouldn't know Malik's smile, or Hudson's heart, or Rey's strength, or Fig's humor, or Jaclyn's quirks, or Savannah's confidence.

"Adults are in charge of our lives," she went on, "but that doesn't mean they're always right. Broadway Bounders can cancel the show, but they can't cancel us!" Her friends shuffled to the edge of the couch. "Our show is bigger than us. Bigger than the JCC. Bigger than Broadway Bounders. Bigger than New Jersey itself!" She paused. "So. Who wants to go rogue with me?"

Before Nat could blink, Hudson's hand shot up, and this time he wasn't grabbing for a cookie. Savannah slapped her thighs. Fig and Jaclyn gave her a standing ovation. Rey did a set of lunges. Malik waved a cookie in the air and shouted, "Who cares who else is on board! WE are on board! Let's get this train going!" He smiled his big, warm smile at Nat, and she tingled.

Rey lifted open Nat's laptop and scanned her basically empty chart. "So, wait—what's the plan?"

Nat giggled self-consciously. "We're going to have to come up with that together."

"Clearly," Rey teased.

"First we should talk about space," Nat decided.

Savannah clinked her thermos with a metal straw. "Well, I have family friends who have family friends who work in the industry," she said. "I'm going to email them now with the subject 'URGENT EMERGENCY.' "

Nat smiled with gratitude, her fingers on her keys. "So, once that comes through, *if* that comes through, we have major jobs to fill. Let's start with director."

"I nominate Hudson," Rey said, tackling him with a bear hug. "He knows the choreography and the blocking and can definitely make up the rest."

Hudson playfully pushed her off. "You can't freak out if I infuse Beyoncé moves."

Fig suddenly slapped Nat's worn couch cushion, struck with an idea. "My older brother is in a band! If we can convince him our show is good exposure, I bet he'll play piano for us and have his bandmates be the pit."

"High school musicians? Yes, please," Savannah said, taking a break from typing on her phone. "Also, I can be on costumes. It'll be easier if everyone's responsible for their own getup, but I'm happy to be the head of the yay-nay committee, just to ensure everything fits the Ozian style."

"I can gather props," Malik offered. "The script has a list of recommended ones in the back."

"I'll stage-manage," Rey said.

"I'll do set design and painting," Jaclyn said. "I'm in advanced art, and my cousin works at Home Depot."

"Aiden would probably like to design the lighting," Malik said.

"I can launch us on social media," Nat said, "and post pictures and quotes from the show."

"Also, Caitlin and Erica quit, so we need a new Midwife and Chistery," Jaclyn said.

"I nominate Nicole for Midwife," Rey said. "She's maternal. She has a bed of dolls."

"I think Leeza would be a master Chistery," Jaclyn said. "She's always talking about how scared she is of the flying monkeys. Becoming one will help her overcome her fear!"

"Great," Nat said, typing it into the doc.

After another fifteen minutes of sorting out the logistics, Savannah suddenly screamed, "OMIGOD, I GOT A RESPONSE!" She thrust her phone into the air. "Everyone, shut up, I'm going to read it."

"No one is talking," Fig said.

"QUIET IN THE HOUSE! 'Hi, Savannah. I don't know if you remember me, but my name is Ronnie.' Nope, I don't. 'Your mom and my mom were in the same sorority at the University of Maryland, where I just graduated.' Go Terps! 'Anyway, your email got forwarded to me since I'm now the box-office manager of Cat's Cradle Black Box Theater in Saddle Stream, New Jersey.' Omigodomigod. 'We, too, are in quite the predicament. We were hosting two weeks of original one-act shows, but the theater company renting the space found out that some of the one-acts have already been published by Samuel French, which disqualifies them. They've withdrawn the show, leaving us with nothing but the deposit. We are hoping to fill the space immediately.' "

Savannah looked up. "Promising, huh? I think it sounds—"

"Don't stop now!" Malik broke in. "Keep reading!"

"Savannah, GOOOO!" Hudson shouted over Malik.

"Okay, omigod." Her eyes dropped back to her phone. " 'We can offer a discounted rate for the use of the space for two weeks of rehearsals, plus a full weekend of performances, so long as you give the theater eighty percent of ticket-sale revenue.' " Savannah looked up again. "Is this a scam?"

"NO! I DUNNO! KEEP READING!" Rey yelled.

" 'We also have a team of summer interns with not enough to do, so they can provide the adult supervision.' "

"Pfff. We don't need babysitters," Fig said, his finger up his nose.

" 'Please give me a ring at the theater before five, and we can sort out the details. Stay great. Sincerely, Ronnie.' " Savannah leaped up from the couch. "Should I text him? Should I call him?"

"CALL HIM!" everyone screamed.

Nat vibrated with excitement but also nerves. In the time that Savannah had read the email, she'd looked up the theater, but the outdated website only featured the shows from last season and nothing about the building itself. "It's accessible, right?" she asked Savannah.

"They have an elevator, yeah," Savannah replied, pressing the ringing phone to her ear. "I saw a production of *Peter Pan* there, and I remember they do."

"Awesome, okay," Nat said.

"Hi, is this Ronnie?" Savannah asked gingerly, springing into the kitchen.

Hudson and Malik high-fived. Fig shoved three cookies into his mouth.

"Don't celebrate yet," Rey warned. "This might cost us."

"We're getting a discount, though," Malik protested.

"The discount could be five percent," Rey said. "The theater rental could be a hundred thousand dollars. We have no idea."

"I have forty-seven dollars in my savings account," Fig offered. "The rest of my bar mitzvah money is in stocks."

"I have a hundred and twenty bucks in babysitting money," Rey said. "But I was saving up for singing lessons."

"I have ten dollars," Hudson said. "My brothers raid my piggy bank."

"I think we need to *fundraise*," Nat clarified. "Not pool our personal money together."

Her friends buzzed in thought. Rey stretched her calf muscles against the couch. Hudson stared at Nat's powered-off TV. Fig ran his fingers down his face. Malik picked at his calluses. And then, suddenly, Warbucks bounded into the living room and smashed his paws against the window. He began barking at a squirrel, and it was desperate and high stakes and loud, and somehow it triggered the ideas to pour in faster than Nat could type.

"We could sell the tomatoes from my dad's garden."

"We could throw a barbecue and sell hot dogs."

"We could do a trivia night—winner takes all, or, *er*, half."

"We could do BINGO."

"A casino night."

"A raffle!"

"Wait, wait," Nat said, her fingers flying on the keys. "Is there a situation where we don't have to give away a chunk of the money we raise, and we also don't have to invest in a product to give away or sell?"

"A KICKSTARTER!" Rey shouted, jumping into the air and nearly knocking over Nat's mom's Tiffany lamp. "My uncle put one together for the documentary film he was making about artificial intelligence in the workplace, and the universe just threw money at him."

"You think the universe will throw money at us?" Malik asked.

"Well, our parents might," Hudson said.

"There are always random people online who want to support good causes," Fig said.

Rey nodded in agreement. "So, my uncle gave out prizes as an incentive. Like robot-related swag: mouse pads, laptop covers, robot bobbleheads. My parents donated fifty bucks, I remember, and that got us tickets to the movie premiere and keyboard cleaner."

"Yeah, but what kind of swag would we give out?" Malik asked. "And wouldn't that add up, too?"

"BROADWAY KARAOKE!" Hudson screamed. "We can do it at my place. I have a machine."

Fig scoffed. "From when, the nineties? We don't need a machine if you've got adapters and laptops or a smart TV."

"I've got *everything*," Hudson said.

"And your family will be cool with it?" Rey asked him. "Like, your jock brothers?"

"My dad is taking them to lacrosse camp in Maine this weekend. It's just me and my mom, and she's trying to be more supportive of my interest in the arts, so I'll be able to guilt her into hosting one hundred percent. I'll text her now."

Fig leaned over Nat's shoulder. "Can I see your laptop for a sec?" Nat handed it over, and he pulled up Kickstarter and started to set up an account.

"I don't get the plan," Malik said. "We sing Broadway karaoke and also try to get our community to donate money to us online? How do those ideas connect?"

Not lifting his eyes from the screen or his fingers from the keys, Fig answered, "The party's just the cast and crew. We pledge to livestream karaoke renditions of any musical song of choice, sung by any of the Broadway Bounders performers, for those who donate five dollars and up on the Kickstarter page."

"YAAAAAAS!" Hudson cried. "But fifteen and up."

"Twenty and up," Malik said.

"One hundred and up," Rey said.

"Hmm, let's do twenty-five," Nat suggested.

"Twenty-five is great," Fig said, offering Nat a fist bump.

"Okay, my mom is in for this Saturday night," Hudson said, holding up his phone, littered with Heart Eyes emoji. "She is trying to show me she loves me."

Just then, Savannah came sprinting in from the kitchen. "So, I'm not saying I'm a miracle, but what I just pulled together is nothing short of miraculous."

Hudson rose to his feet in fifth position. "We got the black box?"

Savannah shrugged proudly. "We needed a deposit of two hundred dollars, which has already been taken care of by my grandparents, who are flying in for the show. You're welcome."

"And the rate?" Fig asked, the cursor blinking where he was ready to type in their Kickstarter goal.

"An additional eight hundred bucks."

Everyone looked at Fig, trying to gauge if that fee was doable. Nonplussed, he typed in the goal—eight hundred dollars—then closed the laptop, his face splitting into a grin. "Done."

Everyone jumped up and exploded in cheers. "*WICK-ED, WICK-ED, WICK-ED!*"

"Gather up bios and song suggestions from the cast," Fig continued, air-swiping invisible dollar bills from his palms, "and we'll be ready to rumble!"

KICKSTARTER: SAVE *WICKED*!!!

Savannah Alexis has been acting, singing, and dancing since she was three years old. Select credits include Zaneeta Shinn in *The Music Man*, Bet in *Oliver!*, and Sally Soda Pop in *Hank & Gretchen*. She dedicates her performance to her supportive parents and Smile Wide Talent.

Sample: "So Much Better" —*Legally Blonde*

Jaclyn Arazi is a skateboard lover. Shout out to the Crescendo Gals, her school's a cappella group. Her favorite role she's played is Mary Poppins. This show will be performed in memory of Sally Bowles. May you defy gravity and float to heaven, sweet rodent.

Sample: "I'd Rather Be Me" —*Mean Girls*

Natalie Beacon is a New Jersey transplant who just moved from San Francisco. She's pumped beyond to be a part of her FIRST. SHOW. EVER! Singing is her life, and if every *Jeopardy!* category was musical theater, she'd qualify and win a billion dollars.

Sample: "There's a Fine, Fine Line" —*Avenue Q*

Reyna Joshi is interested in psychology for the sake of donations from her parents. She is a big fan of truffle mac 'n' cheese. Catch her on the hockey field if you wanna get pucked!!!

Sample: "Don't Rain on My Parade" —*Funny Girl*

Eli "Fig" Newton is a self-taught ambidextrian, fluent in pig latin. He's been lauded as "spincredible" at the dreidel. He looks forward to serving jury duty one day. He once owned an iguana named Taza—green, four feet. She ran away. DM him if you find her. #findtaza

Sample: "Run, Freedom, Run!" —*Urinetown*

Hudson Tucker-Stone is a danceaholic. He has seven pairs of suspenders. "Willing suspension of disbelief, people!" —Me, this one time at Nat's house

Sample: "Dulcinea" —*Man of La Mancha*

Malik Young hails from Pittsburgh but moved to NJ when he was seven. He loves performing and hopes one day to record his own album. He can shoot a hoop and slap a bass. Check out his YouTube channel—coming soon!

Sample: "Suppertime" —*You're a Good Man, Charlie Brown*

CHAPTER FIFTEEN

Superboy and the Invisible Girl

Nat pushed up the cobblestone path to Hudson's front door and pressed the intercom. *Bzzz!* The door swung open.

"Nat!" Hudson looked at the covered plate on her lap. He peeled back the tinfoil, examining a cupcake. Two striped straws topped with chocolate slippers like upside-down Wicked Witch legs protruded from purple frosting. "Did you make these?"

"I did," Nat said, grinning. "My mom helped. And Pinterest."

"I'm very impressed and hungry."

Nat rolled inside and took in Hudson's house, which felt like being in her mom's favorite TV show, *Downton Abbey*, but with sports paraphernalia instead of Victorian art. The foyer was the size of three living rooms, and its ceiling was a skylight. A grand spiral staircase connected floating floors. A giant family portrait hung on the wall. The Tucker-Stone guys were in matching tuxedos, framing the mom with jazz hands.

Hudson caught her staring. "My mom loves it. My dad loves whatever my mom loves. My brothers won't invite friends over because of it. Win. Win. Win." Hudson waved her on, and they followed the floor's vibrations to the packed living room, where Fig had set up a DJ station behind a built-in bar. Instead of beer, Avi was serving Throat Coat tea. "Fig Juice," Hudson said to Fig, "can you show Nat what's up?"

"Oh, hey, Nat," Fig said, swinging around a laptop to reveal the Kickstarter page. The requests from donors were steadily rolling in: "On My Own" from *Les Misérables*, "Corner of the Sky" from *Pippin*, "Fly, Fly Away" from *Catch Me If You Can*, "Nothing" from *A Chorus Line*, "Ring of Keys" from *Fun Home* . . . "So far, the requests are just from our parents," Fig explained. "But I'm hoping we go viral."

"Like, in Saddle Stream?"

"Like, in the world."

Fig went back to work, and Nat feverishly texted her parents, "Donate now! Something from Ham, plz! I'll pay you back when I'm famous!" But before she could add a Money-Mouth Face emoji, she got sidetracked by Malik's vibrato, which was messily making its way through the

Newsies ballad, "Santa Fe." He was in the corner staring at a flat-screen TV, where a YouTube karaoke version of the song was playing.

He was like a magnet. Nat couldn't wait to say hi. Well, first she'd let him finish his song. She smoothed her floral summer dress over her legs and weaved past Steven and Kyle, Leeza and Gia, and Marti and Kyra, and was only a few feet from Malik when she was scratch-attacked by pink crinoline.

It was Savannah, dressed like a cupcake, going in for a hug. "Sorry, my bat mitzvah dress is unruly," she whispered. "Hi. Okay. So. This party is my chance. Malik can finally see me, all fancy, in a nonprofessional light. You *have to* talk to him."

Nat held in a helpless groan. "I'll try later if I—"

"Like now."

"I dunno, Savannah. I have no idea what I'd say."

"Just say, 'Omigod. Savannah looks like Glinda even IRL. She's positively gorg.' Then look across the room at me while I arrange those ugly cupcakes so they look less ugly."

"I made those."

"He's finishing. Get in there, girl! Thanks, love ya!" She scampered away to the table of desserts and watched Nat like a hawk. *Great.* Nat was going to have to do this. She'd say it fast, no big deal, and hope Malik paid her absolutely no mind. It would be fine. Probably. Maybe.

Malik's voice cracked on his final "Santa Fe!" *Aw.* It was actually kind of sweet. He'd get it next time.

"GO!" Savannah overmouthed, waving like a deranged traffic cop.

Jeez. Nat rolled up beside Malik as he cued "One Song Glory" for Petey. "Hey, nice singing," she told him, trying not to stare at his sculpted arms. "It's a perfect song for you."

"Is it?" Malik tossed his dreads over his eyes. "Your ears aren't bleeding?"

"My ears are very happy. You sounded so good the whole song!"

Savannah had somehow migrated from the cupcakes to the tea bar. She poofed out her dress and forcibly giggled to herself, then stared *Do it* daggers at Nat. Tonight's rom-com was turning into a horror film.

"What're you looking—?" Malik went to turn around.

"Savannah is here!" Nat blurted, stopping him. "She, um, looks gorg."

"Like a gorge?"

"Yeah, positively. Like Glinda in real life."

Before Malik could so much as raise an eyebrow, Savannah pummeled between them and flipped her hair, the ends slapping Nat in the face. Her lips moved toward his left cheek—"Mwah!"—then right cheek—"Mwah!" Then she pawed at his shoulder. "You look a-ma-zing. You sounded a-ma-zing, too. Such a Newsie, I love it!"

"Thanks!" Malik said with a shy smile, gently kicking the toe of his sneaker into the floor. "I've just gotta warm up for that last note."

Note to self: Never do any favors for Savannah again. Her heart burying itself in another organ, Nat pushed toward the couch, where Jaclyn was stringing together block letters to spell BROADWAY BOUNDERS. "Can I help?" Nat asked her, desperate for a distraction. "Please let me help."

"Yeah, this is so Zen," Jaclyn said, handing her a thin blue ribbon. "If you hold this up, I'm going to knot the letters in place so they stay evenly spaced."

The job of holding up a ribbon was mindless, so Nat's mind wandered back to Malik. So did her eyes. Savannah was feeding him her cupcake.

"Yo, Natty Nat," Jaclyn said, "can you hold it up higher?"

"Oh, sure."

"Shoots and ladders," Jaclyn said, assessing the banner. "The 'R' is upside down."

Nat lowered the ribbon for Jaclyn and caught sight of Hudson's mom sauntering down the grand staircase, wearing a T-shirt that read PROUD MOM in rainbow stripes. "HUDSON RIVERS," she called, pronouncing "Rivers" like "Rivahs."

Heads turned. Hudson jumped out from behind the bar, his eyes halfway out of their sockets. "Not my name, Ma!" he called back, clearly mortified.

"But it's your stage name, love."

"*Was* my stage name five years ago. Before I learned that the Hudson River is an actual body of water. Ha!"

Nat watched them talk. Hudson was somehow stiff and animated all at once. His mom looked down at her shirt, pinching the Gay Pride message out for emphasis. She eventually rolled her eyes and went back upstairs with a huff, presumably to change.

"It's one thing to be out to you guys," he mumbled as he passed Nat. "I don't need it broadcast over the internet if my mom accidentally slips into the frame."

"I get that."

"Also, she's never actually told me she's proud of me. Maybe we should start there."

Hudson looped back to the bar to organize the incoming requests, and Nat noticed Malik was no longer by the TV. He was across the room, helping set up the "stage"—a corner of the living room arranged to look like a theater-themed photo booth. He and Savannah were draping red velvet fabric like a curtain. Aiden was lighting it with iPhone flashlights.

"Ready?" Jaclyn asked Nat.

"Oh. Sure."

They brought over the sign to hang up. At the same time, Rey came crashing out of the bathroom in a vibrant blue and mint-green sari. "My sister donated fifty buckaroos!"

she cried to Nat. "I'm going to sing 'Elephant Love Medley' from *Moulin Rouge!* all by myself!"

"Yes! Great choice, and WOW: You look beautiful."

"Thanks! My parents bought me this sari for my cousin's wedding this year, but it was kinda pricey, so they made me swear I would find another occasion to wear it, and now I have!" She twisted her hips and her chandelier earrings sparkled from underneath her jet-black locks. "Any requests for you?"

Nat slipped her phone from her dress pocket. *Oh no.* She'd never sent the text to her parents. Smiley Face. Drama Masks. *Whoosh.* "Working on it. We'll see."

Just then, the lights dimmed, and Fig's voice came through the living room's sound system. "Listen up, Wickedy-Wicks," he said from the stage, holding a wireless mic. "Our parents are helping, but if we want to reach Asia, Australia, Oz, and beyond, we're gonna need to do better. Go on Instagram, Snapchat, whatever—and spread the word. If someone shares this fundraising event and tags three rich people who can afford to donate the equiv of a few Subway footlongs, then we will sing their request for FREE. I repeat, FREEEEE!" He spun, his thumbs tucked under the thick straps of his tank top. "First performance in five."

"*THANK YOU, FIVE,*" the room chanted. Then everyone buried their faces in their phones. Nat stared at hers for a couple of reluctant seconds and composed another message. "Hey, Chlo! What's up? Donate plz!" She texted the fundraiser deets and attached the Kickstarter link. Three dots appeared, lighting up and graying. Then they disappeared. Eventually, her screen went black from inactivity, and she was staring at her own reflection.

"Okay, everyone, WE'RE STARTING," Fig shouted. "Malik, take your place onstage! Jac, you're on deck!"

Malik stepped onto a painter's-taped X and studied the TV as the background track of "Santa Fe" blasted through the speakers. Positioned in front of him was an iPhone on a tripod, which was livestreaming to the Kickstarter page displayed on Fig's laptop. He started singing, holding the wireless mic in one hand and with the other hand jammed in his jeans pocket, which made him look reflective. Nat could totally see him as a teenager in 1899 with a dream to escape the city limits. He portrayed the *Newsies* character in his voice, on his face, and through the tension in his bare arms. Savannah randomly screamed a "Woo!" in the middle of the second verse, and Malik was so in character, he didn't even look her way. His warm brown eyes stayed focused at least six feet above the couch as he nailed the final note in his head voice. ". . . *Santa Fe!*"

The party went wild, and Nat did everything she could to keep from physically swooning.

"All right, all right, all right," Fig said, getting into the frame and winking at the camera. "Next up is Jac to the whack! Marti G., you're on deck."

Jaclyn performed "Quiet" from *Matilda* in an alarmingly loud belt. Marti sang "The Hills Are Alive" from *The Sound of Music* while holding up her iPad with images of the German Alps. Nicole cried through "Let It Go" from *Frozen*, but only because her tear ducts activated whenever she sang. Avi charmed everyone with his rendition of "One Jump Ahead" from *Aladdin*. Savannah sang "Show Off" from *The Drowsy Chaperone*, high-kicking and splitting in her platform sandals. It wasn't until Hudson started singing "Summertime" from *Porgy and Bess*, an operatic song for a Black woman that no one had requested, that things took a turn.

"This isn't an open mic!" Nicole complained. "Requests only!"

"It's my party, and I'll sing if I want to," Hudson clapped back.

"You're going to break some glass," Marti whined.

"Well, it's MY glass," Hudson sassed, then sweetly shouted into the mic, "RHONDA TUCKER-STONE? CAN YOU DONATE TWENTY-FIVE DOLLARS, PLEASE?"

"SURE THING, HUDDY BABY," Hudson's mom shouted back.

"THANK YOU LOVE YOU." He flipped the mic in the air and just barely caught it. "It's Miscast now, people!" He winked at Nat. "From this point on—alert your parents, alert your friends—we are only accepting songs we would

NEVER EVER get cast to sing. Capisce?" Hudson thrust the mic toward the audience.

"Capisce," everyone sort of said.

"Say it with enthusiasm! Like the Wicked Witch is dead!"

"CAPISCE!"

As Hudson went on singing, Nat flicked her phone awake—no text back from Chloe or her parents. She scanned the room, wondering who else hadn't gotten any requests. Kyra, Steven, and Jayden hadn't. Gia hadn't. Actually, Gia had co-sung "Sixteen Going on Seventeen," which was Aiden's request.

"Oh, and when u donate, PICK HAMILTON!" she texted Chloe. Three Hearts. *Whoosh.*

Hudson's rendition of "Summertime" faded to completion, and like magic, Fig announced, "This next one's for Nat. It's 'Alexander Hamilton' from the obscure flop *Hamilton.*"

Nat's upper body shot up. "YES! YES!" she shouted. "Who wants in?"

At least a dozen hands went up.

"What part do *you* want to play?" Fig asked her.

"Um . . ." Obviously Eliza. But were they still following the Miscast rule? Because according to some directors, like Calvin, she'd be miscast in any able-bodied role.

"I'm playing Eliza," Hudson butted in. "This is Miscast, people! I know you want to play Eliza, Natty, but you'd be the perfect Eliza, so . . . you're A dot Ham."

"I'm playing Alexander Hamilton?" she asked giddily.

"Yes, sir. Malik, you're Burr."

"That's the opposite of miscasting," Malik said.

"Cry me a Hudson River," Hudson said. "Nat, cast the rest."

Nat looked around at the wiggling raised hands and made some gut decisions. "Nicole, you're John Laurens. Avi, you're Thomas Jefferson. Marti, you're James Madison. Rey, you're George Washington. Savannah, you're Angelica. Fig, you're Peggy."

"Dang," Malik said. "Can't believe you know all the characters off the top of your head."

"Just you wait," Nat replied coyly.

The party rumbled and roared, "Oooooooh, snap!"

Fig played the music. Malik started on the stage alone, and then as each cast member rapped their solo, they entered the camera's frame. Everyone—the actors, the audience—snapped through the song until the final "*Alexander Hamilton*" lyric, when Nat, center, shot her pointer finger straight in the air, just like the show poster.

"Thank you sooooo much! Love ya miss ya!" she texted Chloe.

"I liked your Alexander," Malik told Nat, offering his handshake-slap-snap. "It was fun playing Burr to your Ham."

"Same!" Nat could feel her confidence shoot up in her

chest. She'd just performed *Hamilton* with the cutest, sweetest, most talented guy she'd ever met.

Feeling light-headed with adrenaline, Nat grabbed some Throat Coat tea as Fig began announcing the next song. The sound system suddenly recalibrated for "Can You Feel the Love Tonight" from *The Lion King*, and Malik took his place back on the X.

"So, who's the Simba to your Nala, my man?" Fig asked Malik.

He scanned the party. His eyes melted into Nat's eyes, and he smiled. *Me? I'm your Simba?!* She gripped her wheels, ready to join him AGAIN, this time as his feline boyfriend for the most romantic Broadway duet of all time.

"Savannah," Malik said.

"Savannah!" Fig called.

Savannah?! Nooooooooooo. Nat nearly spat out her tea. Had Nat made Malik think she didn't like him? Had she pushed him and Savannah together? Or had he liked Savannah all along? Malik and Savannah started singing, their mouths on either side of the microphone. Nat didn't want to watch. She couldn't help but watch. Their voices blended like a banana-berry smoothie. With a lot of sweet eye contact. It was torture.

Nat's phone dinged, and she seized the opportunity to leave the living room. She pushed past the foyer and into the dining room, then pulled her phone from her pocket.

It was a text from Chloe. "Are u being sarcastic??"

"Ha, no," Nat texted back with a heart. "U picked Ham, right?"

"No."

"Oh, sry! Was prob my dad!"

"Prob."

Chloe had used no exclamation marks. No emojis. Just a couple of cold, hard periods. *Is she mad at me?* Nat wondered. *No. It's not like I've done anything wrong.* Sure, lately she and Chloe had been a little *off.* But that was normal: Nat had moved across the country. She was settling in. Chloe was settling in without her. It was summer. They missed each other.

"You sound mad," Nat impulsively texted.

"U have no idea what i sound like cuz u haven't heard my voice in like a week."

Nat's heart twisted. *Okay, so maybe I did do something wrong.* Before she could think it through, she was calling Chloe. It rang twice.

"Hey," Chloe answered flatly.

"Hey," Nat said carefully. "So, um, what's up?"

"Nothing much." She paused long and hard. "You?"

"Um, well, I'm at a fundraising party for *Wicked* because the show got canceled, and Malik is singing a love song with Savannah, so that really sucks. Can you hear it?"

"No."

She doesn't get it. Just tell her the JCC BURNED DOWN. "So, it's been really hectic—"

"I don't care."

Nat full stopped. "What—what do you mean?"

"I don't care about Malik or Savannah or any of your new friends."

"*Okay* . . ."

"Also, twenty-five dollars is a lot. Maybe not to you, but to me it is. And to get that text after I haven't heard from you in over a week?!"

"I haven't heard from YOU! You're always with Beatrice."

"I'm allowed to make friends, Nat."

"Okay, but, with *her*?!"

Nat's breathing was heavy in her throat. The dining room's crystal chandelier was a blinding blur. She was losing her best friend. Malik and Savannah were still singing in the background and probably falling in love. At a party full of people, Nat felt so alone.

"I gotta go," Chloe said.

"Wait, Chlo—" Dial tone.

Nat pushed toward the living room, feeling like a zombie—dead and directionless. Malik and Savannah were smiling at each other through the instrumental break.

"Kiss! Kiss!" heckled Steven.

"Guys, stop!" giggled Savannah.

Nat's heart started to crack.

She guessed they were a couple now: Malik and Savannah. Their mash-up name would be Malannah. No, Savik. They'd go on a date later this week. Sushi. They'd share California rolls, Nat's favorite. By the end of the summer, they'd go into the city and walk around Central Park. Their parents would give them money to rush a Broadway show. In the darkness of the last row of the theater, they'd share their first kiss.

Malik and Savannah sang the last chorus and their chemistry was on fire. *How delusional have you been?* Nat asked herself. *You've never had a boyfriend or shared a kiss, and there's a reason for it.* She squeezed her eyes shut and tried to picture Malik slow dancing with her, sweeping her off her feet, taking her into the city. She couldn't see how, logistically, any of it would work. The fairy tales, the romantic comedies, the books, the TV episodes about love—nobody looked like her. No love interest was in a chair. She didn't exist. And if she couldn't picture doing couple things with Malik, how could she expect Malik to?

Savannah had been right. *He could be that boy, but I'm not that girl.*

"HELLO, ACTORS!" Hudson's mom suddenly shouted from the living room entranceway, wearing a silk robe over yoga pants. "So glad you were able to express yourselves tonight, but three separate neighbors have called to complain about the noise." She nodded at Hudson, standing beside her. "Huddy?"

"We sound amazing. Our neighbors should be *paying us*. Anyway, through Kickstarter donations, we've raised . . ." He *sloooowly* opened an envelope and pulled out nothing. "Just kidding. Kickstarter doesn't spontaneously mail results. It's all online. We've raised $1,260!!! Hooray!!! Now go home!"

CHAPTER SIXTEEN

Going Down

Nat dawdled outside the building complex where the Cat's Cradle Black Box Theater was housed. For the first time since she'd gotten into the show, she was dreading rehearsal. She'd maybe gotten three hours of sleep the night before. All she could think about was how her chance with Malik had passed, or about how maybe she'd never had a chance with him at all. The moments when she'd been able to push Malik out of her head, her fight with Chloe had pushed right in. She hated that Chloe was mad at her. She hated that Malik and Savannah were probably now a pair.

Nat blew out a loud sigh. It was fine. Maybe everything happened for a reason. She shouldn't let a boy distract her from her acting career, anyway. Plus, if Malik did like Savannah over her, then he was not worth the heartache.

Fig pushed the door open for her. He must've caught her hanging outside like a weirdo. Nat forced herself to roll inside.

"Hey," she said, pushing between Hudson and Rey with a strained smile on her face. No one responded. She darted her eyes around the lobby, where, oddly, the cast was gathered. "Are we waiting for everyone before we go up?"

"*Well* . . ." Hudson said, his eyes kind of glazed over. "It's complicated."

They were on the ground level. The black box was on the sixth floor. "Complicated" could mean only one thing. She scanned the space until she spotted the elevator in the far-left corner of the lobby. There was a sign on it: OUT OF ORDER.

"But—but—" Nat stammered as her heart dropped. "When is it getting fixed?"

"It's not," Savannah said. "I mean, *eventually*, but it's not really urgent for them."

"Why isn't it urgent for them?" Nat asked.

Savannah flippantly shrugged. "How am I supposed to know?"

"Because you're the one who recommended this place. You're the one with the family-friend hookup."

"Chill," she replied. "I'm sure someone can carry you up."

"I definitely can," Malik offered.

"Or Rey," Savannah said.

"Yeah, I can carry you up," Rey offered. "Like I've said before, you're really light."

"I don't want to be carried up," Nat said, trying to keep her voice from breaking. "Thanks, but it's a hassle, and a big responsibility, and I don't want to have to rely on you guys every single rehearsal and show."

"*Okay*," Savannah said, slowly cocking her head. "Well, honestly, it's not like you have much of a choice."

"That's *why* I don't want to be carried up," Nat snapped. She looked around into the silence. Chins were pointing down. Eyes were being averted. "You guys should go up."

"So, you'll hop on my back?" Malik asked.

Nat's mind flashed to the retreat. She was so stupid to think that their piggyback ride had meant something. She was so stupid to think her new friends understood her.

"Or Rey's?" Malik offered. "Whatever you want."

"No, it's okay," Nat croaked.

"So, um, how are you going to get up?" Jaclyn asked.

"I'm not." She wished the lobby wasn't an echo chamber. She wished the whole cast wasn't crammed together, listening. "I've told some of you guys—remember? I don't like feeling stuck. If the elevator is broken, if there's no way I can get up and down on my own, then I can't do the musical."

"This isn't the bus," Savannah said. "This is the *actual show*."

"Exactly."

"You're being really melodramatic."

"I'm really not." Her face on fire, Nat suddenly stormed toward the door. She pushed it open, but it slammed back into her chair before she could make it through. Her friends rushed over, their hands outstretched, waiting for her permission to help. Without it, they probably feared getting snapped at again. It was fine. She could do it on her own. She shoved open the door with enough force to exit, and then, déjà vu, she was outside by herself. Again.

A lonely reject.

There were pricks behind her eyes, and they were stabbing quick and hard. *How did this happen? Will stuff like this ever stop happening to me?* Nat turned her head to look back through the ground-level window, but between her tear-blurred vision and the distance, she couldn't tell if the cast was shifting awkwardly, unsure of what to do, or if they were already climbing up the stairs, moving on without her.

Whatever. It didn't matter. What was done was done.

Nat reached into her pocket and pulled out her phone. A tear splashed onto the screen. She rubbed her phone dry on her shorts, only to have another tear splash onto it, then another. She wiped her eyes with her fists, but the tears kept spilling. She held the phone up from her soaked lap, her finger hovering over her mom's contact. *Ugh.* She really didn't want to call her mom and have to tell her she'd been right all along.

She opened the Uber app, punched in her address, and opted for the wheelchair-accessible ride. Five minutes.

There was nothing but a parking lot in front of her. A car irresponsibly sped by, its hot exhaust blowing her tearstained cheeks dry. She could hear the building door creak open behind her. Maybe Hudson was about to come out. Or Rey. Or Malik. She didn't want to talk to any of them while looking like a hot mess. She blotted her face with the bottom of her T-shirt as if that would mask the lumps in her throat, and then Savannah, of all people, tapped her on the shoulder. "Hey, are you okay? You don't have to quit over this, if that's even what you're doing."

Nat pushed herself backward, away, her heart thumping like mad. "How long has the elevator been out?"

Savannah scoffed. "I don't know."

"Yes, you do!"

"Fine. A month."

"A *month*?!"

"It's a really good performance space, Nat," Savannah said, gripping the roots of her hair. "I literally don't understand why you're being like this. Now everyone's inside feeling super guilty, but we don't have another option."

"Why not?" Nat fired back. "We were only supposed to look at accessible options."

"Well, sorry. Stuff happens. You adapt."

"You're telling *me* about adapting? Are you kidding? Why am I the one who always has to adapt? Why don't YOU adapt?" Nat shook her head so hard she could feel the veins in her neck twist. "Do you have any idea what it feels like to work on a show, *to revive a show*, only to find out that you can't physically get into the theater?"

"I do have an idea," Savannah muttered, tearing up like *she* was the victim. "I do understand."

"Sure," Nat said.

"I do."

Her Uber pulled up, and Nat laser-focused her attention on Ramón, the driver. He was friendly. He unfolded a ramp from his trunk so she didn't have to get out of her chair. She rolled up the back with a push from Ramón, and he strapped down her wheels.

Savannah stood there watching, arms crossed over her chest, helpless.

"This okay?" Ramón asked.

"Yeah, it's great," Nat replied. "Thank you."

He gently shut the back door, and they were off.

CHAPTER SEVENTEEN

Raise You Up

Nat had her wet face buried in a pillow when she heard her mom's two soft knocks. She wasn't audibly crying, but Warbucks was, nudging the back of her head with his nose. *Get it together*, she told herself. She sat up, wiping away fresh tears with the back of her hand. "Come in," she croaked.

Her mom slipped into the room. One look at her face, and Nat just crumbled. She collapsed back into her pillows, and the tears came flying out of her eyes. It didn't matter anymore. She was done trying to prove herself. Her parents were right. She had never been fit to be in the show.

Nat's mom climbed onto the bed and pulled Nat into her chest. "What happened, Natty?"

"The theater—has a broken—elevator, so I quit," Nat told her between sobs.

"Oh, Natty, I'm so sorry." She sighed and pulled Nat in tighter. "That's awful about the theater. Why didn't you call me to pick you up?"

"Because I didn't want you to think I was helpless."

"*Helpless?!*" Her mom shook her head in little bursts. "I don't think that!"

"Of course you do!"

"Honey, listen to me: You're not helpless! You got into the show on your own! You made new friends! And then, when there was a fire, you rallied your castmates to keep going!"

"Then why are you always so overprotective of me?!"

Her mom held Nat's face in her hands. "Because I love you, and I can't help but assess the risks you take. It's my job! And you take A LOT of risks!"

Nat sputtered a laugh.

"Natty, I'm so proud of you and your persistence. I've been so impressed. You can't give up now."

"What?!" Nat wriggled out of her mom's hand sandwich. "I thought you didn't want me to be in the show!"

"Baby, I didn't want you to get hurt. But now I've seen how happy the show has made you, and it's by *not* doing the show that you'll get hurt."

Nat sniffled, and then more tears flew out of her eyes. "What's the math on that?" she joked.

Nat's mom smiled. "I think the math is strong."

Nat took a moment to wrap her head around everything her mom had just said. She *wanted* Nat to do theater because it made her happy. She was *proud of her* for taking so many chances to follow her dream. "Thanks," Nat told her after a few seconds. "Now I *really* wish the theater was accessible—"

Nat was silenced by the sudden, increasingly loud pounding of sneakers. Warbucks howled as her bedroom door cracked open and three heads popped in—Hudson's, Rey's, Fig's—like stacked turtles. Behind them were Malik, Savannah, and Jaclyn. "Your back door was open—don't call the cops," Hudson blurted.

"It's fine," Nat's mom said warmly, waving them in. "Nat, do you want me to . . ."

"I'm good. You can, um . . . It's fine."

Her mom understood. "I'll be in the kitchen if anyone needs anything." She gave Nat a kiss on her head and left past the Oz Bounderz. They piled into the room with Warbucks weaving between them, licking legs.

"We are seriously sorry," Malik said. "We had no idea about the elevator."

Hudson got down on his knees. "Natalie Schuyler Beacon, we refuse to do the show without you."

"My middle name is Joy, but—"

"OF COURSE IT IS," Rey said.

Hudson inched closer to Nat, but Warbucks toppled him. "If you don't do the show, none of us will do the show!" he declared amid a slobber attack.

"Honestly, it's only fair," Jaclyn said. "If it weren't for you, we would have all just moved on with our lives, very sadly."

"Truth," Malik said.

"I mean, no elevator?" Fig added. "How could Cat's Cradle ever lift us up as performers?"

"I'm borrowing a pillow," Jaclyn told Nat, then used it to smack Fig's back.

Nat cracked a smile, then sighed. "It's nice of you guys to come here, but aren't we going to lose a lot of money if we drop the theater?"

"Only the two-hundred-dollar deposit," Savannah answered, picking at her fingernail. "It's fine. I called and canceled already. So."

"Oh. That's—" Good news, except now their only standing offer was Nat's backyard.

"Don't worry," Malik reassured Nat, practically reading her mind. "We WILL find a new theater."

"Definitely," said Rey. "We'll call schools, churches, camps . . ."

"Town halls, gated communities, fifty-five-plus communities . . ." said Hudson.

"Temple Judea, Temple Beth Am," said Fig.

"All the temples," said Jaclyn.

"I dunno . . ." Nat hesitated. "Don't worry about me. Maybe you can redeposit the deposit. It just feels late to try to get the show up and running *again.*"

"It's not," Malik countered. He held up his copy of the *Wicked* book from Nat's bedside table. "Elphaba is slammed with challenge after challenge. She too feels majorly defeated, and then she—"

"Turns it all around!" Jaclyn broke in.

"Fakes her death to escape her enemies," Malik corrected.

"Same thing," Jaclyn said.

Malik went on. "My point is: Elphaba thinks outside the box. Nat, are you just gonna give up? Or are you gonna channel Elphaba and join us as we do whatever it takes to keep *Wicked* alive?! Like you said: 'Our show is bigger than us.' "

"Bigger than the JCC," said Hudson.

"Bigger than Broadway Bounders," said Rey.

"Bigger than New Jersey itself!" said Fig.

Malik tossed the book at Nat, and she caught it against her chest. The warmth of his hands was still on the cover. "Come on," Malik pleaded. "Are you with us?"

"Can I just—?" Nat reached for Hudson's hand on her left and Rey's hand on her right. The hyper, charged energy in the room evaporated into super-mush. Or, at least, that's how Nat was feeling—super-mushy—as she watched Malik take Hudson's hand and Jaclyn take Malik's hand and Fig take Jaclyn's hand and Savannah take Fig's hand and Rey take Savannah's. Warbucks was in the center of the circle. It looked like they were about to do a séance to communicate with his Labrador and poodle ancestors.

"Somebody say something, please," Savannah urged. "This silent prayer circle is freaking me out."

"I was just trying to thank you guys," Nat admitted. "I have no idea what we're doing."

"Whatever—your answer is?" Malik pressed.

Nat took in a slow breath. "Let's. Get. Wicked!"

"WOOOOOOOOOOO!" they all screamed in celebration. They smashed into a group hug. Confined in the middle and excited by all the excitement was Warbucks, chasing his own tail.

"Oz Bounderz fo' LIFE!" Fig shouted.

"Oz Bounderz fo' LIFE!" everyone shouted back.

Nat's heart grew two sizes. No, three.

After all the camaraderie, it was time to say goodbye. The group disbanded, but Savannah lingered in Nat's doorway. It was quiet, and the air between them quickly grew thick with awkwardness.

"I was really rude to you," Savannah finally said, picking at a split end.

Nat's heart chugged, wondering if it was too rude to agree.

"Malik and I have been best friends—well, not *best friends*—but close friends for three years," she plowed on. "And last summer, I had a really huge crush on him. But nothing happened. So I thought this summer, if I showed him I was into him, we'd have a chance. But then you came along."

"I don't think Malik *likes* me," Nat said.

"Well, he doesn't like me," Savannah mumbled. "At least not like that."

"But what about at the party? When he picked you to sing 'Can You Feel the Love Tonight'?"

"Oh, *that* night? Malik only picked me because, three years ago, Broadway Bounders did *The Lion King*, and I played Young Nala. It was a shout-out to me."

"Oh. Are you sure it was just a shout-out?"

"I'm sure. That night, he also told me he's happy we're friends. But, like, 'just friends.' So yeah." Savannah plucked the hair she'd been picking at, and in the silence that followed, all Nat could hear was the monster-pounding of her own heart. "Anyway, after talking to my therapist about it, I realized that I was acting out against you because I was . . . *jealous.* You two have something real, and after a while, I felt, I dunno, threatened or whatever."

"Wow." Nat was shocked and ecstatic—she and Malik *did* have something real after all!—but she didn't want to rub it in by pushing for more details. "You see a therapist?" she asked instead.

"It's not a big deal," Savannah replied curtly, playing with her elbow skin. "A lot of people go to therapy. It's not weird."

"I know. In California, I saw a therapist, too."

"Oh." Savannah's arms fell to her sides. "So you get it, then."

Nat nodded, petting Warbucks. "He's my support dog, actually."

Savannah's face brightened. "That's soooo cute! I asked my parents for a support dog, but my sister is allergic, and even though I was like, 'Cockapoos are hypoallergenic,' my parents vetoed the pet thing altogether."

"That stinks," Nat said. "Maybe one day they'll give in."

"Do you know that most dogs in LA are support dogs? Celebrities have a lot of anxiety. I read a lot of magazines."

"Me too." Nat wanted to correct her—most dogs, even in Hollywood, were probably not support dogs—but there were more important things to discuss. "I'm low-key into *Popstar!*" she shared instead.

"I'm high-key into *Popstar!*" Savannah cried, clapping. She sifted through her pink Herschel backpack and pulled out the latest edition. "Have you read this one—about hair products that have been tested on rabbits?"

"I haven't."

"It's inhumane. *Inanimale*. I'm leaving this with you so you can cross-compare your gel."

"Thanks," Nat said. "So, anyway—"

"OMIGOD!" Savannah's jaw dropped so fast, the rubber bands in her braces nearly snapped. She raced over to the mirrored closet. It was open a crack, exposing the wheels of Eliza Hamilton. "Is this the Little Dipper made by Colours Wheelchairs?!"

Um. Nat's head whirled in confusion. "You know that *how*?"

"My little sister has the same one." She gave Nat a shrug of admission. "She has CP, which is short for—"

"Cerebral palsy, I know. My best friend Chloe has it." Nat rolled over to her desk and pointed at the picture of the two of them at the beach. "She's not in a chair, though. She walks with canes."

"There you are reading *Popstar!*"

"Yeah." Nat's heart started to ache. She was mad at Chloe. Confused by Chloe. She wished Chloe were in her room right now instead of Savannah.

Savannah sank to the floor and leaned her head against the closet doors. She was back at her split ends. "Can I be honest?" she asked quietly.

"Of course."

"Being around you reminds me of my sister. I've always been really protective of her." She leaned over her straightened legs and gripped her toes. "Like, when we were in elementary school, I would sometimes see her out at recess, sitting alone on the blacktop while all the other kids were running around. I would leave my friends to hang out with her."

Nat nodded emptily. After everything Savannah had put her through, her compassion was hard to picture.

"So, when I first met you, I was like, 'Yay! A connection!'

I even asked you to talk to Malik for me because I thought it would make you feel included and cool. But then, after you danced for Calvin, I realized you didn't need me to protect you or to make you feel cool. And it hit me that Malik was probably crushing on *you*, not me, and after that, I didn't really know how to treat you."

Bewildered, Nat wheeled closer. "You could have just treated me like how you treat everybody else."

"I wanted to. I told you I understood where you were coming from."

"But, Savannah—what you did with the theater was really messed up. How would your sister feel if you'd pulled that on her?"

"I would NEVER have done it on purpose." Savannah's chin started to quiver. Her cheeks reddened, and her eyes glassed over. "I picked the black box, remembering there was an elevator. I literally found out this morning that it had been out. I should have checked before, like you'd asked, but I'm sorry—I didn't." She blinked, and a tear spilled from the corner of her eye. "You shouldn't have to choose between the show and feeling stuck. You're right."

Now Nat started to choke up. She waved Savannah to her bed and transferred next to her.

"I've seen my sister feel stuck," Savannah went on, her voice shaking. "She wanted singing lessons with my voice teacher, but she works out of her house, which is on the third floor of a two-family home. My sister didn't like my mom carrying her up, either. She said it made her feel like a baby."

Nat offered Savannah her fuzzy pink pillow. She hugged it to her chest.

"One time, the lift in the school cafeteria was broken for an entire month, and my sister had to eat in the nurse's office every day. She needs me, and I don't know how to help her."

"Independence is really important," Nat said.

Savannah looked up, her eyeliner spiraling down her cheeks. "What do you mean?"

"Having control makes me feel normal," Nat explained. "The less I have to lean on people for support, the better I feel about myself."

"So, then, how do I help her with that?"

Nat gnawed on her lip as she thought about all she'd done in the past few weeks. "Maybe if you give your sister some space, she'll surprise you."

Savannah balked. "I can't just randomly leave her to fend for herself."

"No, I mean, encourage her to put herself in situations where she can be more independent. She'll learn how to do stuff on her own. Like, at the JCC, there was an elevator and a ramp backstage. Sure, I'd sometimes ask Rey for a push, but I could basically access the whole theater. Or, like, when I used to wheelchair race—" All of a sudden, Nat froze.

"What?" Savannah asked. "Nat, what's wrong?"

"Wow, I think I— That would be . . . WOW!"

"You're scaring me."

"I've got the perfect theater!" Nat said, breaking into a grin. "I've got the perfect theater for our show!!!"

Hi Shira,

My name is Natalie Beacon, and I was given your contact info by Cynthia Abrogar, the coach of the Lightning Wheels. I am writing to you on behalf of Broadway Bounders—check us out online! We are a group of tweens who are looking to book a theater space for a low-budget production of *Wicked*—we are in a bit of a jam because our space at the JCC burned down.

You have an AMAZING theater in the sports building by the track. Is it available this summer? If so, what is the rental rate? We would take really good care of it, we promise. We are really responsible, good kids with big dreams, big talent, and big hearts.

Thank you so much,
Nat Beacon, age 13

P.S. If you feel more comfortable coordinating with an adult, I can loop in my dad, Jeffrey Beacon. He's the new athletic director at Saddle Stream High School.

CHAPTER EIGHTEEN

The Shoe Fits

Nat led her castmates through Redker's College's sports building toward the theater, her heart thumping with anticipation.

"I have a lot of anxiety right now," Hudson said as a pack of football players charged past. "Why are they invading our space?"

"I think we're invading theirs," Malik said.

"The football field and track are behind the building," Nat explained. "The college built a performing-arts wing on another campus, so now the theater is used for conferences and stuff."

"And you just, like, found this place?" Rey asked.

"Sort of. I was about to race here when I found the *Wicked* flyer." Now Nat was feeling anxious. It had taken a lot of guts to reach out to Coach Cynthia—not with the intention to rejoin the team but to ask about the theater. Turns out, she was way friendlier over email than in person.

"It's fate," Savannah said. "I just wish they had the original show dates free."

"Yeah, I was hoping that, too," Nat said, wincing apologetically. "But they have a statewide track conference here starting Friday, and then after next weekend there are sports orientations."

"My grandpa can't come now," Savannah whined. "He's flying in from Florida tonight but flies back on Tuesday."

"We're livestreaming it, so your grandpa can definitely watch," Fig said.

"He's having cataract surgery on both eyes next week."

"Maybe he can just listen?" Nat asked.

"His hearing aids are broken."

"Ignore her," Hudson whispered to Nat. "Everyone's on board with the new schedule. Obviously, we could use the extra week."

"Thanks," she whispered back, finally arriving at the theater. "Anyway, this is it!" She pushed open the double doors, and the space was just as she'd remembered it—a neat proscenium with a red velvet curtain cloaking the stage. Traditional, intimate, real. *Please like it*, she prayed as the cast spilled inside.

"I LOVE THE CURTAIN!" Savannah exclaimed, skipping down the aisle to the stage. Nicole and Marti followed her and then started coughing.

"It's a little dusty," Nat warned.

"I can bring in my dad's leaf blower," Rey offered.

"Sixty seats!" Fig hollered from the stage, pointing at the empty audience.

"Everyone'll fit?" Nat asked him.

"The JCC seats one-ninety-nine, but we never sell out. Better to have a small space and fill it."

Rey stomped around behind the back row. "We can always do standing room," she said. "At least eleven bodies can fit here comfortably."

"I say twenty, and we pack 'em in like sardines," Aiden said. He yanked a metal tab at the foot of the stage, exposing a storage space with multicolored wires and lighting equipment. "Jackpot!"

"It feels very black box in here," Gia said, running her fingers along the wall.

"Except black boxes are black and a box," Savannah said flatly.

"Fine. It feels very *indie*."

"It feels classic is what it feels like."

Nat sighed with elated relief. "Classic" was the perfect way to describe it. As the cast got settled in the first few rows, she rolled to the aisle of the front row, next to Malik. Malik, who *didn't* like-like Savannah, who had an obvious connection with Nat, and who might be smelling the vanilla deodorant she'd applied to her wrists as makeshift perfume.

Hudson clapped three times from center stage, and the cast clapped back. "Thanks for being here, *Wicketeers*!" he said. "We raised the funds, Nat is a total badbutt, and here we are, at this *classic* college theater—"

"NO!" Rey shouted at her phone from the foot of the stage. She began feverishly texting.

Hudson shot her a *Chill out* look. "*Anyway*," he went on, "we will spend the next ten days rehearsing and running tech, and then we open next Friday. In order for this to work, everyone's gotta be an actor and a part of the production team. If you're not in charge of something backstage, we need extra help with the set, costumes, and—"

"Hey, Hud?" Rey pulled herself up onto the stage and began whispering and smacking her phone. Nat watched Hudson press his arms tensely to his sides and tear at his cuticles.

"What's going on?" Malik asked Nat.

"No idea," she answered.

Rey shuffled aside in a stupor, and Hudson's face was drained a ghostly gray. "I need the senior members of the show for a quick backstage conference," he called with a twitchy smile. "Everyone else, um, hang tight. Actually, warm up. Nicole—you play the piano. Can you lead vocals?"

"I guess," Nicole said. "Which—?"

"Whichever. You're the man."

"I'm a girl."

"Girl power!" With that, he and Rey punched the curtain to find the opening. A billow of dust enveloped them as they disappeared backstage.

Nat watched Savannah, Fig, Marti, and Avi rise from their seats. "That's us," Malik said to Nat, already standing beside her. "Senior members are anyone going into eighth grade."

"Oh, cool." Nat wheeled to a ramp at the left foot of the stage, and Malik gave her a pull. They passed through the break in the curtain, and backstage would have been pitch-black if it weren't for Fig's iPhone flashlight beaming around like a disco ball.

"Ew, it's so creepy back here," Savannah said.

Fig pretended to seize. "I'm being mauled by the ghost of Macbeth! He wants to be king of Redker's College!"

Savannah palmed Fig's face. "You're not supposed to say the M-word in a theater, you moron!"

"M-word."

Rey whistled with her fingers in her mouth, and everybody hushed. "Jaclyn is a no-show," she said. "I called—straight to voicemail. Then I got a text." She thrust out her phone, and everyone lurched forward to read the screen.

"That's Candy Crush," Savannah said flatly.

"Oh, whoops." Rey swiped out of the game and simply read the text. " 'Heyo, Rey. Some devastating news. Now that the show is "student run" and is diff dates, my parents are making me go to my stepcousin's bar mitzvah in Wisconsin.' "

"Wisconsin?!" Marti exclaimed. "That's so far!"

"Yeah," Rey said. "So, I wrote, 'Oh, no! You'll be back for Monday's rehearsal?' She wrote, 'Nope. Pensive face. Loudly crying face. Star of David.' "

"We open next Friday," Savannah blurted. "Please tell me our ELPHABA will be back on Tuesday. Wednesday, the latest."

Rey narrowed her eyes. "Well, I wrote, 'When will you be back?' and she wrote, 'I won't be.' And then—"

Savannah shrieked, "SHE WON'T BE BACK?!"

"Let her finish!" Fig said, shoving a hand over Savannah's mouth. "Rey, go!"

"No, she won't be back," Rey confirmed, stuffing her phone back into her khaki shorts. "She's going to be in Wisconsin for the next three weeks."

The senior cast members broke into freaked-out murmurs.

"Nat, you're one hundred percent sure the space isn't available later?" Malik asked.

She was sure. She wished she weren't. "They told me it's next weekend or not at all."

The cast on the other side of the curtain began warming up in harmony—"*Bumble bee, bumble bee, bumble bee, bumble bee!*"—and Nat fell into a guilty panic. This was all her fault. Had they stuck with Cat's Cradle, they could have kept their original show dates, and Jaclyn could have convinced her family to stay. She was the star of the show. *Irreplaceable*. Nat was in the ensemble. *Very replaceable*. In fact, the production would be easier without her involved. She knew it. Everyone had to be thinking it.

"Um, um," Hudson said, pacing. "What if Rey plays Elphaba?"

The whites of everyone's eyes darted around the dark. Nat looked at Rey, expecting her to be ecstatic, but she was chewing her thumb in terror. "I dunno, Hudson. Nessa is my first actual part, and I barely deserved it. Elphaba? I mean . . ."

"Let's just say you, theoretically, jumped in for Elphaba," Fig said. "Who would play Nessarose?"

"Nat," Rey replied.

Suddenly, backstage was spinning, and Nat's heart was slamming against its walls. "You think I can play Nessa? What about the part where she walks?"

Malik jumped in. "We can figure that— Oh! We can switch up the dialogue and lyrics so that Nessarose can stay in her chair."

"That's illegal," Savannah declared. "Unless you wanna call Stephen Schwartz and negotiate a rewrite."

"WILLING SUSPENSION OF DISBELIEF!" Hudson yelled, heel-tapping. "We don't need to *change the script*. When the lines say Nessarose walks, and Nat doesn't, the audience will just imagine it!"

Yes! Yes! Yes! Nat's heart jolted upward until Savannah balked. "*Wicked* is about witchcraft, magic, and fantasy," she said. "If the audience doesn't see Nessarose walk, we're not honoring the material. It'll look like we're putting on a DIY show."

"Well, it *is* a DIY show," Malik argued.

"Nessarose getting to walk is a *significant* plot point."

"Then we'll have her 'walk' offstage," Malik said. "Like how in Greek tragedies the deaths happen behind the scenes."

"It's not just about the *moment* Nessarose first walks," Savannah said. "She walks for a huge chunk of act two."

"Then we CGI it."

"This is *live theater*, Malik, not Hollywood!"

Everyone was cringing. Nat's heart had exploded out of her body and was dead on the floor. Of course, onstage, she could never play a character with a disability that gets fixed. She would never be fixed. She wasn't a witch. Life wasn't magic. If anyone other than Nat understood that, it was Savannah.

"Can everyone stop freaking out and listen?" Savannah huffed. "The solution is obvious."

Nat bet Savannah was going to suggest that Marti or one of the younger kids play Nessa. Or that she play Glinda *and* Elphaba herself, turning the show into some sort of experimental theater piece.

"No offense, Rey," Savannah said, then locked eyes with Nat. "Nat needs to play Elphaba."

Wait, what?! "ARE YOU HIGH ON GREEN ELIXIR?" Nat *might* have screamed with giddy shock. She did. She did scream it.

"It's obvious," Savannah went on. "We've all heard Nat sing. She has the strongest belt. She works harder than anyone. She knows the whole show like the back of her hand." She grinned at Nat. "Plus, Nat and I are already frenemies. Real-life Glinda and Elphaba."

"Frenemies how?" Fig asked Savannah.

"It's between Nat and me, Fig. Just accept what I'm telling you. God."

Her heart beating at triple-overture speed, Nat glanced around the room. She saw only smiles of agreement, Rey's included.

"But how is Nat going to defy gravity?" Fig asked. "I mean, just logistically . . . Not only does Elphaba walk, she flies."

"*Bumble bee, bumble bee, bumble bee, bumble bee!*" The harmonies buzzed, then halted. There was a stinging silence of uncertainty. After a moment, it was broken by Hudson. "If Nat plays Elphaba," he said with unwavering confidence, "trust me, she'll fly like no one has flown before."

CHAPTER NINETEEN

Like a Comet Pulled from Orbit

One more time, Nat told herself. She propped a pillow against her bed's headboard, then cued up the original Broadway cast recording of the Glinda/Elphaba duet, "For Good." She pressed play on her laptop and sang her heart out. "*It well may be that we will never meet again.*"

This had been her routine for the last five days. Mornings in rehearsal. Afternoons translating choreography with Hudson. Nights in her room, practicing her lines and songs. Always, always channeling her inner Idina Menzel. Shower, bed, repeat.

"Woof! Woof!" went Warbucks, nose-nudging her door open and pouncing onto her bed. His paws hit the keyboard, and the song stopped.

"You fluff monster, no!" Nat cried. She kissed his

head, then cued up the song for what had to be the fourteenth time.

Earlier that evening, practicing the harmonies of "What Is This Feeling?" had been a breeze, since Savannah had insisted on running it on repeat all week until they were solid. Per Malik's suggestion, she'd practiced "The Wizard and I" like a monologue, speaking the words to herself in front of the mirror—and that had been really character-connecting. But for some reason, she had not been able to get through "For Good" without messing up.

"*So much of me is made of what I learned from you. You'll be with me, like a handprint on my heart.*" Her voice cracked on "*heart.*" She paused Spotify and started singing her part a cappella. "*Like a ship blown from its mooring by a wind off the sea.*" She tried to focus on her breath. Her jaw relaxation. Her soft palate.

But all she could think about was Chloe.

Her gut laugh that turned into a snort. The fish she'd doodle on the cuffs of her jeans. The way she repeated bad jokes and made them funny. How she had both a fear of heights and a hatred for gravity. How avocado was her life.

"And just to clear the air, I ask forgiveness for the things I've done you blame me for."

Nat closed her eyes, and blues swirled under her lids. When she opened them, tears were running down the sides of her nose. Before she could even think about collecting herself, she was Skyping Chloe.

"Hey," Chloe said stiffly, her face coming into focus. Her olive complexion was masked by a neon-green face peel, and her thick brown hair was twisted into a giant knot at the top of her head. This was bad news. Facials screamed *sleepover party*.

"Are you alone?" Nat asked.

"Yeah," Chloe said. "Are you crying?"

"Yeah." Nat gave a small chuckle. "I didn't think you'd actually pick up."

"Me neither."

"But . . . you're okay to talk now?"

Chloe shrugged. That was a start. Nat's heart started to pound as mushy words swished around in her head. *I love you. I miss you. We have so many inside jokes. We have so many memories.* "Since when do you do face peels?" she asked instead.

Chloe shrugged again. *Since Beatrice. That's when.*

Nat rubbed Warbucks's belly, averting her eyes. "Are you still mad at me?"

"It's not that I'm *mad* at you," Chloe said. "It's just . . ." Nat's fingers got caught in a matted part of Warbucks's fur. She untangled the fur as she watched Chloe puff out her cheeks and exhale. "When you left, Natty, I felt alone and scared."

"Wait, you did?"

"Duh. We hadn't been apart since nursery school. I know it's a lot to move across the country, but at least you were getting the chance to start fresh." Chloe self-consciously tugged at the sleeves of her terrycloth robe. "I knew you'd meet new, amazing friends. You're, like, a friend magnet: pretty, so cool, and confident." She sped up. "Did you ever think about how hard it would be for me to make new friends, staying in the same town with the same people I've known my whole life?"

Not really. "But you did make friends, right?" Nat asked, trying to be positive. "You're friends with Beatrice?"

"Sure."

"Well, that's good."

"Is it? Because you don't make me feel like it is."

Pow—Nat felt a gut punch of guilt. "I just didn't expect the two of you to click," Nat explained. "I'm glad you do, but—"

"I walk with canes," Chloe cut in. "It's not as if I had to fight off all the people looking to fill your slot. My summer instantly sucked without you. But then Beatrice got into a huge fight with Jeanine and Lauren, and she was desperate. And since I was desperate . . ."

"You shouldn't have to feel desperate."

"Whatever I felt, I felt. I know Beatrice isn't the world's greatest friend. But I can't just stop being friends with her, because then I'll go back to feeling invisible." Her voice broke on "invisible," and her eyes turned to wet glass.

"I—I don't know what to say. I just seriously had no idea."

"Think about it. I might not have shown it, but of course as soon as I found out you were moving, I was a mess. Kids leave me a ton of space to walk, like I have leprosy. No one talks to me, or if they do, they speak really slowly, like my brain is as wobbly as my legs. All the boys we think are cute will never, ever think I'm cute back." The wetness in her eyes wavered over the brim, and then tears started streaming down her face. "With you by my side, I've managed okay, but without you? I worried I'd have no one to talk to or laugh with ever again— Ugh, I'm getting green on my robe."

"You wanna clean it? You can call me back later . . ."

"I'll just tie-dye it."

Nat watched Chloe blot her cheeks with the back of her hand, wanting to tell her that she was the opposite of invisible. She lit up a room. She was ridiculously corny, and hilarious, and smart, and real. One day, the perfect cute guy would come along, and he'd think she was just as perfect and cute. She was the best, and anyone who'd ever made her feel less than that was a loser. But instead, Nat's curiosity took the lead with another question. "Why did you act so happy about my family's move?" she asked. "If you were, you know, so *unhappy*?"

Chloe shrugged guiltily. "Your parents asked me to put on a brave face. They said, 'to make the transition easier for you.'"

"Wait, what?!" Nat said so loudly she startled Warbucks to all fours. "So you *pretended* to be excited about it just because my parents asked you to?"

"Yeah, sorry."

"Don't be sorry. *They* should be sorry! They shouldn't have done that to you. To me! I only shared good stuff with you because you seemed so okay with me moving. I didn't mean to make you feel bad."

"I know, Natty. I was sad, but I kept it in because I didn't want to be a bad friend."

Nat wished she could reach across the screen and give Chloe the biggest, longest hug, but since that was impossible, she'd have to battle the lumps in her throat to speak. "Chloe, I'm so sorry," she said. "You're the coolest, strongest girl. I know that sounds lovey and mushy, but—"

"No. I mean, it does, but *go on*."

"You're my best friend. You deserve to be happy and to feel good about yourself because you're the most amazing person I've ever met."

Chloe sniffled. "I'm blushing under the green—you just can't see it."

Nat laughed a little. "Is it almost time for—" Chloe's phone alarm rang. It was set to "California Girls." They really were in sync.

"That's fifteen minutes!" Chloe said, then went at the green goop, peeling it from her chin, her cheeks, up the bridge of her nose, and her forehead. "Ta-da!" She flung the face mask off-screen. "How do I look?"

She had about a quarter of the mask still plastered to her face. The exposed skin was blotchy and red. "Like a beautiful swamp."

"That's exactly what I was going for!"

"Obviously."

"Bathroom break. Hang on."

Nat felt a bubble of happy relief bounce around her insides. She wanted to make up for lost time. To ask Chloe all about her beach trips, her summer reading, her brothers, her life. But then Chloe's canes came into the frame.

"THEY'RE NEW!" Nat screamed.

"Yup!"

"THEY'RE PINK!"

"Yup! Like . . ."

"Like?" Nat asked. "Oh! Like Peaches?"

"LIKE PEACHES!" Chloe squealed.

"They have to meet."

"They're meeting now."

"No, like, wheel to footpad," Nat said. "Where have you taken them?"

"Willy's Deli, Fort Point, Golden Gate Park, Teen Acrobatics—"

"Teen Acro-*whaaaaa*?"

"Batics," Chloe said. "I've been flying all summer long."

"Um, you're afraid of heights."

"Not anymore! Remember when you called me, and I was in the park bathroom? I was trying to tell you about it, but you were going on about a casting email you wanted me to forward."

"I'm a jerkface."

"No, and, Nat, honestly, I do care about you and your show and your new friends. Did you say something about it being canceled?"

"It *was* canceled, but now it's back on, and I'm playing Elphaba, the lead—"

Chloe screamed. "YOU'RE PLAYING *THE LEAD*?"

"Uh-huh. I've been practicing the songs twenty-four seven. No idea how I'm going to fly yet, but—"

"YOU HAVE TO FLY?"

"Ha, yeah. Elphaba's the Wicked Witch of the West, and at the end of act one, she flies up on her broomstick!"

"Oh. My. God. Are you singing with Malik, too? You have to tell me EVERYTHING!"

Nat launched into the whole story and then listened as Chloe told hers. They went back and forth like a ping-pong rally, sharing jokes and laughs at a speed faster than anyone else could have comprehended. It didn't matter that they were separated by 2,928 miles or by their screens. Nat could close her eyes, and it was as if Chloe were curled up on her bed beside her.

When it was finally time for Chloe to eat dinner, Nat shut her laptop. Her head ached, thinking about what her parents had done. She rolled through the bathroom and knocked on their bedroom door.

"Nat? Come on in, hon," her mom said.

"No, Mandy, I'm—" her dad started.

Nat opened the door and saw her mom on her bed, peering over her book, *In Pursuit of the Unknown*. Her dad was sweating, assembling a new wheelchair. "Ah! Natty, you're not supposed to have seen this yet!"

"Sorry." She hesitated. "What, um, is it?"

"It's a tennis chair. For you to play tennis in! Happy opening night . . . almost."

Nat's anger dissolved, leaving her feeling guilty and confused. "I just—"

"What's wrong?" her mom asked. "What happened?"

"You make it so hard to be mad at you," she said. "But I am. Mad at you."

"Okaaay," her mom said.

"You told Chloe not to show me how sad she was about the move? Why would you do that?"

Nat's mom closed her book and rubbed her eyes. "Sweetie, that was just me being a parent."

"No, that's not an excuse!"

Her mom choked a sigh. "I'm—I'm sorry."

"We thought Chloe could handle it," her dad explained, "and it would make the move less hurtful for you."

"That wasn't fair to Chloe, and it wasn't fair to me. You need to trust me!"

"We do," Nat's mom insisted.

"So then give me space."

"Natty—" her dad started.

"I depend on you both for a lot of stuff," Nat plowed on. "And I get that I'll need help forever. But that means you need to let me try out independence whenever I can. I need to test the limits, and I want your support."

Her parents, seemingly stunned, nodded.

Nat took a deep breath. She stared at the gray wall for a few calming seconds and then said to her dad, "I know when I turned down racing, that was hard for you."

Her dad cocked his chin. "You mean I've been driving you to Redker's for something other than racing?"

"Ha," she said. "But you should know I'm happy here. In this house. With my friends. So the move hasn't been all that hurtful." She watched her dad's eyes well up. "Are you crying?"

"It's sweat. Jeez."

"You're definitely crying."

Nat's mom put her arms out toward Nat. "Come here, baby." Nat rolled to the bed and transferred on top of the comforter. "Eleven years ago, when the accident happened—"

"Mom, you don't have to."

"I thought it was the end, but, God, it was just the beginning. We are so proud of you, Natalie. Watching you blossom into a strong, independent—" She cut herself off as her eyes began welling up, too. "It's been the most rewarding, incredible experience." Nat's mom pressed her forehead against Nat's forehead, eyes closed, and they were connected by the warmth and wetness of their faces. Nat's dad joined the mush party, squeezing Nat so hard it was more like a wrestling hold than a hug.

"I'm gonna throw up my pasta, ow!" Nat said, giggling. "You stink!" Her dad just squeezed tighter. Then Warbucks leaped onto the bed and covered her with slobbery kisses, and there was nothing she could do to stop it. "Ew, ew!"

"What's the *Wicked* song that would go here, Natty, if this moment were a musical?" her dad asked, finally releasing her. " 'Put on a Happy Face'?"

Nat groaned. "That's from *Bye Bye Birdie*."

" 'One Small Girl'?"

"That's from *Once on This Island*."

" 'For Good'?"

"Wait, how do you know that?"

Nat's dad scrunched his shoulders with a goofy smile.

"You were singing it on repeat," Nat's mom said. "Your belt travels. Also, *please*, you've been listening to *Wicked* since you were a little girl."

"*Because I knew you*," Nat's dad sang completely off-pitch, "*I have been changed for good.*"

CHAPTER TWENTY

Tomorrow Is

"Elphie, Glinda, Guards—PLACES!" Hudson called as the cast chaotically scrambled through the stage fog. "This is our only dress rehearsal before tomorrow's opening and we're not supposed to stop the show at all. So let's do the flying part again, and NOT STOP, please!"

From the back of the house, Aiden flicked on the spotlight. It mistakenly hit Gia, who was peeking out from backstage with her finger in her nose. Then it swirled around and landed on Nat's left. She rolled into the light.

"Hey, Nat, let the light follow you, 'kay?" Rey said.

"Okay, sure," Nat said, finding it best to just go with the flow. Tech Week was *intense.*

A backdrop fell. It was the Ozdust Ballroom. "Wrong scene, Kyra!" Hudson called.

"I know, but I'm a palace guard in this scene, so I can't— Petey!"

"On it!" Petey cried. He dropped a different backdrop:

a swirly neon-green one with an ominous Roman numeral clock that Nat had helped paint.

Suddenly, an enormous shadow was cast over it. It was Savannah in an oversized wedding dress. "Sav?" Hudson said through clenched teeth. "This *might* work as the bubble dress, but what was wrong with the other white costume here?"

"Why would Glinda wear a white tennis skirt?" Savannah challenged him. "She doesn't play tennis in this scene."

"Well, she doesn't get married, either."

"Did you *buy* a wedding dress?" Rey asked.

"Borrowed. Also, *testing, testing one, two, three*," she sang. "My microphone sounds lower than Nat's."

"That's on purpose!" Steven called from the foot of the stage, loading fresh batteries in the other body mics.

"I shouldn't be punished because I project!" Savannah protested.

"I'm kidding—fixing it."

"All right, are we ready, Bounders?" Rey asked with strained pep.

"READY!" the cast responded.

With a snap, Rey cued Fig's older brother, who was conducting his band, School Bell Blues. They'd agreed to be the pit so long as they got to advertise in the playbill for their upcoming gig at a vacant autobody shop. They'd only first looked through the sheet music that morning, and, well, it showed.

Nat opened her mouth, ready to wail, "*IT'S*—"

"WAIT!" Hudson interrupted. "Is that broomstick a Swiffer?"

Malik sheepishly popped his head out from backstage. "It was that or my mom's vacuum. And she was vacuuming when I left, so—"

Hudson shut him down with an *I will melt you* stare.

"Yup, yup. I'll get a broom for tomorrow. Carry on."

The music swelled with dissonance, and the cast scurried back into their places. They'd stop-started so many times, Nat's soft palate was more stretched than it had ever been in her life. "*IT'S MEEEEEEE!!!!*" she wailed, raising the Swiffer in the air. "*And if I'm flying solo, at least I'm flying free . . .*" As she pushed downstage with one hand, her castmates crouched into squats. The backdrop was replaced with one that was nearly identical, except the clock was small and closer to the floor, painted to give the perspective that Nat was flying high. "*To those who'd ground me, take a message back from me . . .*"

Nicole turned on a fan to make Nat's cloak "blow in the wind," but it just blew Nat's witch hat off—straight into Savannah's face.

"Ow!" she yelped.

Leeza and Kyle drew the curtain so that Nat could belt her final notes alone on the fog-cloaked stage, but Savannah was staggering in front of her, clutching her nose.

"OKAY! CUT! STOP!" Hudson shouted. "WE WILL FIGURE OUT THIS CLUSTERMUCK LATER!"

"Am I bleeding?!" Savannah screeched, pinching her nose. "I feel blood everywhere!"

"There's no blood," Rey said. "I'm getting you ice."

"LET'S TAKE TEN FOR INTERMISSION," Hudson went on, "AND THEN WE'LL RUN ACT TWO—NO STOPPING!"

Mortified, Nat started to roll offstage, when the spotlight dissolved, and the house lights snapped on. Her pupils wigged out. She thought she was seeing pink canes in the back of the theater. She rubbed her eyes, then opened them. Yup, those were definitely pink canes. "HOLY *SMOKEY JOE'S CAFÉ*!!!"

"HOLY *SHOW BOAT*!!!" Chloe called. "That's a musical, right?"

"Yes, it is, but wait! This is UNREAL!"

"YUP!"

"You're HERE!"

"YUP!"

They met midway in front of the stage and crashed into each other for the BEST. HUG. EVER.

"How are you— What are you doing here?!" Nat asked, letting go.

"Your parents. They flew me out."

"Ah! Okay, my parents *can be* awesome. Is that weird to say about my own parents?"

"Not weird!" her dad said, jogging toward them with a camping pack on his back. "Very not weird."

Nat threw her arms around his waist. "Thank you, thank you!"

"We messed up. This is our apology."

Hearing "messed up," Nat cringed. She peeled herself off her dad and asked Chloe, "You didn't happen to see the act one finale just now, did you?"

"I did," Chloe admitted. "You were UNREAL, but the flying part was, um, not flying."

Nat laughed, then shook her head, doubly mortified. "We're working out the kinks. I hope. I dunno. Does it look stupid?"

"Yes."

"CHLOE!"

"What? I'm being honest. In the *actual show*, you said Elphaba flies."

"She does, but trust me, Hudson and I brainstormed ways to make it happen, and this is the best and only option."

Chloe refrained from nodding. "Remember what I did this summer?" she asked.

"The beach? What does that—?"

"The other thing."

Chloe shot Nat's dad an insidery look, and he handed Nat the camping backpack. "Go ahead, open it," he said.

"*Okay*." Curious, Nat pulled out a tangled clump of black straps with a bunch of carabiners attached. "What are . . . ? Wait— Omigod."

She lifted her head, and Hudson was hustling to them, frantically waving his hands. "Hi! Chloe, you're here! Thank Oz. You are saving us from disaster."

What the wizard was happening?! Nat looked at Hudson and then at Chloe, trying to piece it all together. Hudson was detangling the harness. Chloe was clapping her canes in excitement. "You're gonna fly, Natty," she squealed. "You're gonna fly for real!"

Dearest, darlingest Momsies and Popsicles, Friends, Family, and Random non-Ozians who've wandered into this sports facility tonight expecting a lecture on "Focus on the Field,"

We are so honored you are here! This production of *Wicked* has been entirely student run after, "by the winds of chance," a tragic fire destroyed the precious stage and physical memories at the JCC, where Broadway Bounders had held a decade-long residency.

After hearing that the show would be indefinitely postponed, the cast and crew you will see tonight banded together to make the saying "The show must go on" a reality. We raised money. We borrowed costumes. We constructed and painted the set. We did some recasting. And we reworked the blocking and choreography. Now, here we are, ready to take you for a musical ride down our yellow brick road.

We would like to thank Calvin, Lulu, and Cora for their help in getting us started, as well as all the donations of time, money, skills, and space we got from family and friends.

Wicked is a tale of perseverance. It's about doing right, even when it's simpler to do wrong. It's about unlikely friendship and unlikely romance. It's about embracing your own differences and learning from the differences of others. It's about reaching for the stars and settling for nothing. It's about then, and it's about now.

Stay spellbound,
Your ever-grateful *Wicked* cast and crew

CHAPTER TWENTY-ONE

The Most Important Night

Backstage, Nat approached the cast sign-in sheet as the harmonies of "What Is This Feeling?" buzzed in her mouth. She grabbed a pen from a duct-tape pocket on the wall and signed. Name: Nat Beacon Part: Elphaba Time: 6:28 PM. This was it. Tonight was the night.

"Hey," Hudson whispered, popping into the wings. "You're here!"

"Yup! I can't believe we're opening in, like, an hour and a half."

"Ninety-two minutes, yeah. More like ninety-seven. To allow for parking. I set up signs all over town."

"I saw," Nat said, smirking. "And! I still can't get over the fact that you conspired with my parents and Chloe. That was really cool of you."

"It was all Chloe. Your parents gave her my phone number, and she called me up with the best plan ever. I promised you'd fly like no one has flown before, but I had no idea just how true that would be."

Suddenly, a patch of curly emerald hair popped out from behind the curtain.

"Your hair!" Nat exclaimed to Fig. "It's not purple!"

"The purple was fading," Fig said. "It was time."

"This is definitely not fading," Hudson snarked, reaching for a feel.

"Don't touch!" Fig said, dipping backward. "It's still setting."

"Well, it looks incredible," Nat told him.

"Thanks, and check it." Fig pulled a program from his back pocket and handed it to Nat. "My dad's office has an underused color copier."

"This is so legit," Nat said, flipping through. The cover was a mini version of their black, white, and lime-green show poster. The first page was the cast note, followed by bios and headshots. The back hosted advertisements from community shops like Borecky Bros' Bagels and Pia's Pies.

"Pia's Pies!" Nat cried out. "I went there my first night in Saddle Stream. You guys go there?"

"We go everywhere," Hudson answered. "It's a small town. With literally nothing to do."

"Except put on overly ambitious musicals," Fig added.

"Ha!" Nat hugged the program to her chest. "Well, it's perfect—just like the Broadway playbills I've seen online!"

"Online?" Hudson scoffed. "You say that as if you've never seen a Broadway playbill in person."

"I haven't," Nat admitted. "Because I've never seen a Broadway show."

Hudson pliéd, then dropped to the floor. Fig clutched the curls he wasn't supposed to touch.

"Oh, come on!" Nat cried, giggling. "Cut me some slack. I didn't live here until a month ago."

"I'm taking you when our run is over," Hudson said. "We'll snag discounts on TodayTix or wait in line at TKTS."

"I don't know what any of that means."

He placed a finger on her lips. "Shhh. We'll see something extraordinary. Tell no one you're a Broadway virgin."

"My lips are sealed," she mumbled as Rey busted backstage.

"We're starting warm-ups, guys; let's— NAT!" She kissed Nat's cheek, loud and smacky. "What up, what up, my sister from another mister! Get it? Because Nessa and Elphie are sisters with different dads? Holler!" She gulped. "Sorry, I'm nervous."

"It's cool. Me too," Hudson said.

"Me three," Nat said.

"Me eleven," Fig said as he led the way onto the stage. The rest of the cast was "milling and seething," which was theater-speak for when actors randomly walk around, trying to not bump into one another. Nat joined in, trying to keep "soft focus" and not hard focus on Malik, who was walking a path of right angles. In his vintage New Jersey Nets jersey, he looked like an athlete stuck in a Pac-Man game.

"You ready to make your professional debut?" Rey asked Nat as their paths converged.

"This isn't *professional,*" Savannah corrected her, power walking past.

Rey tried again. "You ready to make your Redker's College sports facility debut?"

"Yes!"

Nat rolled along the edge of the stage as Malik swaggered toward her, Fiyero-style. "Hey, Elphie," he said, blowing past. Then he paused, turned around, and winked. "I look forward to debating the politics of Oz with you over coffee, poppy-seed biscotti, and a slow dance."

Nat tried to suppress a giggle. "Smooth," she said.

Milling and seething lasted a few more minutes, and after that, Hudson led a dance warm-up and Fig's brother led vocal warm-ups, inspired by his original music—less Broadway, more heavy metal.

"We're at half hour till the house opens!" Rey announced. "Makeup, hair, costumes—chop, chop to the top, y'all."

The cast retreated to a dressing room, which was actually an old locker room—abandoned jockstraps lay strewn on top of rusting lockers. Nat rolled to a quiet corner, where she put on her costume: a navy blazer, a pleated navy skirt, and prop glasses. Next, she balanced her mom's magnifying mirror and her Ben Nye makeup kit on her lap, and she sponged her face, neck, arms, and hands green. Then she put on Elphaba's combat boots.

Suddenly, Savannah appeared over her.

"Oh! Um, hi!" Nat said, startled.

"This is my sister, Sierra," Savannah said. She stepped out of the way for a girl with blue eyes and stick-straight blond hair that was pulled back by cat ears. She was sporting a *Lion King* T-shirt and fringed black leggings. She was the spitting image of Savannah. Except in a chair. "Sierra, this is Nat."

"Wowsers!" Sierra said with fangirl hysteria, her eyes darting from Nat's green face to the wheels of her chair and back. "You're ELPHABA in the show?!"

"Yup," Nat said, feeling weirdly famous.

"Sierra's a really good singer," Savannah bragged.

Nat watched Sierra light up. "How come you didn't do Broadway Bounders this summer?" she asked her.

Sierra shrugged, her light dimming. "I—I didn't know I could."

Nat nodded with understanding. "What grade are you going into?"

"Sixth," Sierra replied.

"Have you ever performed before?"

"At church. I'm kind of a musical theater dork, though."

Nat chuckled. "Most of my experience is singing in chorus concerts, so I hear you. But you should *definitely* join next year. You've got to!"

"Yeah, you should totally join," Savannah told her sister, smiling encouragingly.

Nat felt the urge to give both of them a giant, squeezy hug, but that seemed too intense, so she offered Sierra a high five instead. A little bit of green smudged onto Sierra's palm. "Whoops, sorry," Nat said.

"I'm never washing my hands again," Sierra overlapped.

"HUDDLE TIME," Hudson shouted. "EVERYONE ONSTAGE IN TWO."

"*THANK YOU, TWO,*" everyone chanted back.

Sierra did a double take.

"You'll catch on," Savannah assured her.

"Yeah," Nat chimed in. "Theater talk will become your talk soon enough."

"Well, I can't wait," Sierra said. "Have the greatest, best show!"

After giving Sierra a bighearted thank-you, Nat wheeled toward the stage, riding high, and nearly knocked into Malik. He was wearing a maroon vest over a billowy white button-down. Her high jumped higher.

"Wow, you look like you were born to play Elphaba," he said.

"And you, Fiyero."

He swung a leather satchel from his back to his hip. "I borrowed the vest from a Catholic school a few towns over, and the shirt is my dad's from the nineties."

"What about the bag?"

"Oh. It's Avi's. Well, his mom's."

"A-mazing."

The cast gathered in a tight huddle onstage and threw their arms around one another's shoulders. Nat put her right arm around Rey's waist and her left arm around Hudson's.

"*Poo-wa-bah,*" Fig chanted softly.

"*Poo-wa-bah,*" everyone chanted in response.

Nat didn't know what "Poo-wa-bah" meant, but she joined in on the next chant. She'd gotten used to following her friends' leads and making sense of nonsensical theater rituals.

The call-and-response built—"*Poo-wa-bah! Poo-wa-bah! POO-WA-BAH!*"—until the cast was shouting it at the top of their lungs and jumping. Nat gripped Rey's and Hudson's costumes and let herself rise and fall. Then everyone's arms flung center, forming a stack of hands. Nat could feel Malik's heart pound against her back. She could taste Savannah's hairspray. She could smell Kyra's natural deodorant. *Oh, the love.*

"Three, two, one!" Fig said.

"*POO-WA-BAH!*" everyone shouted as their hands flew up and out.

Nat giddily wheeled to her opening place, stage right, and tried to resist the urge to peek out through the curtain to find her parents and Chloe. Her stomach swirling like a tornado, she closed her eyes, took a deep breath, and tried to focus on Elphaba: who she was, what she wanted, and how she was going to get it.

"PLACES!" Rey called. "THE HOUSE IS OPENING!"

CHAPTER TWENTY-TWO

What I Was Born to Do

Nat raced onstage for the finale of act one, fleeing the Palace Guards. Her heart was beating so violently, so fast, she thought it might leap out from her lacey black dress—her second costume of the night. As Elphaba, she examined her green fingers, poking out from her long sleeves. Who was she to trust anyone? Who was she to try to make change? Who was she to try anything at all?!

She slipped back into herself for a brief moment, recalling how getting onstage for the first time tonight had been terrifying, but how every entrance after that had gotten easier . . . until this one. This one was making her shake.

"*Elphaba!!!*" Savannah cried, chasing after her. "*Why couldn't you have just stayed calm for once?! Instead of flying off the handle!*"

Nat barricaded a door with Malik's broom as Madame Morrible's hate speech blasted through the speakers: "*This distortion! This repulsion! This Wicked Witch!*"

Nat had heard that line many times in rehearsal, but it had never ceased to twist her insides. Even now, the cruel words latched on to her with such force, they knocked her speechless. Her face burned as the spotlight hit her, and, suddenly, she was outside herself, thrown into a montage of memories, old and new. She was by herself at recess while all her friends were running around, playing tag. She was rolling backward down the steep ramp out of the gymnasium while no one lent a hand. She was struggling to transfer into a minivan for a school trip to the Exploratorium, listening to the impatient moans of her classmates. She was a hassle. She was different. She was alone.

"Don't be afraid," Savannah said as Glinda, crossing behind her. She latched a clear rope to the carabiners on Nat's sagging harness, jerking her upright at the shoulders.

"I'm not," Nat replied as Elphaba, purposefully adjusting her black, pointy hat so that it stood tall on her head. Nat didn't feel tall in her hat. She felt small, like it was shrinking her. Meanwhile, her stomach was rising and dropping. She might throw up.

She beckoned toward the audience. "It's the Wizard who should be afraid. Of me!" The music shifted. "*Something has changed within me. Something is not the same.*" The words—they felt so real and so right. All the lyrics did. They swam in her mouth and projected out with new meaning. She felt like she was singing the song for the first time, discovering herself, coming out from hiding. The broomstick levitated to her, thanks to Fig and his stage magic (invisible string puppeteered from the wings), and she could hear the audience *ooh* and *ah*.

Savannah grabbed the cloak and wrapped it around Nat's trembling shoulders. Then they launched into a harmonious duet. "*I hope you're happy in the end. I hope you're happy, my friend.*" "Friend" was sung in perfect unison.

The Palace Guards burst onstage, their muskets drawn. They dragged Savannah off into the wings as Nat pointed her broomstick at them. "*IT'S NOT HER!*" she screamed. "*IT'S MEEEEE!*" She felt a tug skyward. She was rising up, out of her chair. "*IT'S MEEEEEEE!!!!*" she shouted again on pitch, and she could feel Elphaba's superpowers, her *own* superpowers, pulsing through her veins. She was three feet in the air, five feet in the air, ten feet, fifteen.

High above the neon-green fog, she dropped her jaw and belted, "*So if you care to find me, look to the western sky! As someone told me lately: 'Everyone deserves the chance to fly!'*"

It was scary being up so high. It was terrifying relying on Hudson and her dad in the wings, pulleying her to keep her elevated. The harness was tight against her back, and she worried she'd flip or drop the broomstick or both. There were so many people watching, including her mom, including Chloe. Did the flying look legit? Did *she* look legit?

"And if I'm flying solo, at least I'm flying free . . ." She sang her worries partly away, sick of caring what anyone thought. Right now, she didn't need a wheelchair or a lift or a shower chair or braces or a standing frame or a walker or ANYTHING.

"To those who ground me, take a message back from me . . ." Nat wasn't watching herself anymore. She was back in her own body. Her legs were her legs, and her arms were her arms, and her voice was her voice. The sound was gorgeous and alive, powerful and emotional, soaring and unrestricted. It pierced through the musty theater air, out to the audience, beyond Redker's College, over the New Jersey border, and across the country to California, then skimmed the sea.

"Tell them how I am defying gravity," Nat sang. *"I'm flying high, defying gravity!"* She'd done it. She'd followed her heart. She'd auditioned. And gotten cast. And she was lifted into this role, literally, by friends who believed in her.

"And nobody in all of Oz, no wizard that there is or was, is ever gonna bring me down!"

Not Calvin. Not new kids at school. Not herself. Nobody.

She belted her final riff, *"AHHHHHHHHHH!"* and thrusted the broomstick over her head. The green fog blasted into a blackout. The red curtain closed in front of her. It was intermission.

Nat was Nat. A real actress. In a harness. Getting lowered toward the stage floor. Rey caught her and guided her into Peaches. Hudson detached the rope. Malik handed her a water bottle. Savannah wrapped her arms around her. They were whisper-cheering stuff over one another, like, "Go, Nat! You did it! Dang, you defied gravity! Heck to the yeah!" And for the first time in her entire life, she felt . . . unlimited.

CHAPTER TWENTY-THREE

Because I Knew You

It was 12:11 AM, and Nat was still hanging with her friends in her living room, piled around and on the new couches that had arrived only yesterday. They weren't worn in with memories of back home, but they had new memories imprinted onto them. Especially since Fig had spilled Mountain Dew all over the love seat he was sharing with Savannah and Chloe, and Nicole had left a smear of Ben Nye stage makeup on an arm of the three-seater before she'd gotten picked up.

"I can't believe you dropped Kyra on the dip," Hudson said to Fig, barely glancing up from Chloe's phone, where he and Rey were watching her recording of the show.

"Oh, snap!" Rey said. "*That's* the moment my costume split. I was wheeling across the stage, and then it wasn't until the next scene that I realized my left love handle was getting a lot of oxygen."

"So, what happened?" Nat asked, pushing closer to Rey.

"Marti's sequined wings is what happened. She had safety pins on 'em that kept busting open."

"Aw, turn it up," Savannah said, flapping her arms to quiet the group. "Avi sounds so good on his solo line." As the room hushed, Avi's voice cracked big time. "How did I not hear that during the show?! Ugh, I told him not to eat dairy or bananas! Did he eat dairy or bananas?"

Chloe guiltily raised her hand. "Is that the kid with the bleached-blond mullet? Looks like a surfer?"

"Yes," Savannah replied.

"I thought he was cute, so I gave him my Yoo-hoo."

"CHLOE!" Savannah said, playfully throwing an M&M at her, which fell between the cushions, imprinting on them yet another memory.

Fig whipped out his phone. "I'm texting Avi right now that you derailed his performance."

"Nooooo," Chloe said, giggling. "Say I gave him the Yoo-hoo as a gesture of, uh, my fondness for his hella-good looks."

"California girls be crushin'," Fig joked. "Right, Malik?"

"Huh, yeah," Malik mumbled, distracted. He was hovering over the coffee table and running his pointer finger along the green icing at the edge of a baking pan. "This CAKE, though! You seriously made it?" he asked Nat, shielding himself from Warbucks.

"Without my mom and without Pinterest," Nat said, grinning.

"You put Munchkins on top. I mean, *Munchkins*!"

The cast listened and sang along to a few more numbers on Chloe's phone, and then Hudson handed out copies of the show poster. "For everyone to sign!" he said. "Take a poster, write your name on the back, and then pass it around. Perfect your autograph, people."

"They're for us to put on our bedroom walls," Rey explained to Chloe. "But you can sign mine if you want. You're technically stage crew."

"Oooh, I feel so famous," Chloe said, grabbing a gold Sharpie from Hudson's fist.

"Sign mine first, or I will be deeply offended," Nat joked to Chloe, reaching for a silver Sharpie. Malik went for the same marker, and their hands collided. Then they both let go. The Sharpie dropped to the rug. They both bent over to swipe at it. Their heads banged, and no one got the Sharpie. "Ow," they said in unison, sitting up and breaking into face-eating smiles.

It wasn't long before posters were flopping all over the room, and Chloe agreed to AirDrop the video to everyone, since the signage was so distracting.

"I'm gonna get some air," Malik said as Nat went to pass her poster to him. "Wanna come?"

"Oh, um." Nat looked at Chloe, not wanting to abandon her. But Chloe was now absorbed in a game of Would You Rather? with Fig. She opted to fart loudly every time she had a serious conversation rather than burp after every kiss. She was fine.

Nat transferred into her chair, and Malik followed her as she rolled out to the back deck. He sat on the bench Nat's family had brought from California. Her dad had constructed it out of a fallen giant sequoia, and Nat had helped sand it and give it its protective glaze.

"What a night," Malik said, sighing into the breezeless humidity. "Not a ton of air out here, but still."

"Yeah. In California, the days are hot, but the nights are kind of chilly."

"That sounds nice." Even though they were an arm's length from each other, it felt as though Malik was miles away. "So, you miss the West Coast?" he asked.

"I do," she said, transferring next to him onto the bench. "But the thing I miss most about it is right here."

Malik widened his eyes, then pointed at himself. "Me?"

"No," she giggled. "Chloe!"

"Not that I thought—" He shook his head. "I was just—"

"Do you miss Pittsburgh?" Nat cut in, saving him.

"How do you know I used to live there?"

"Your bio from the Kickstarter page."

"Ah," he said, clicking his tongue against the roof of his mouth. "I do a little. I have a lot of fam there. And my best friend, Dominick. We used to shoot hoops together every summer and sell spiked lemonade, but PG style—spiked with hot sauce."

"Ew—how?!"

"Don't knock it till you've tried it. Sweet, sour, burning. Yum."

"Actually, that sounds kind of delicious. I was quick to judge."

"Yeah, that's you all right," he joked, dropping his hand to the bench and maybe accidentally grazing Nat's fingers. "Always judging."

"Ha."

He kept his hand there. And slower than the slowest ballad, their fingers interwove.

"I really thought you liked Savannah," Nat admitted, ruining the moment.

Malik pulled his hand from hers to smooth out the frizzies in his dreads. "Oh, man. Well, I had *no idea* what you were feeling."

"Oh no!" Nat said. "Maybe that's because I got in my head about you and Savannah, and, like, pictured you two going out for sushi and everything."

"Huh? Nah, I don't eat raw fish or avocado."

"YOU DON'T EAT WHAT?!"

"Okay, Cali girl, chill," he said, chuckling.

"I just— Sorry. Now I'm *really* judging, but I legit didn't know that was possible—to not eat *avocado*?"

"So, I guess we can't make this work, huh?"

"Make what work?"

Malik's mouth rose at the corners as he gazed up at the stars. "I dunno . . ." he said, and Nat had a feeling he did know, and she did, too. But she wasn't about to say it, and clearly, he wasn't, either. So she looked up, also, and spotted the Big Dipper, or maybe it was the Little Dipper.

"Do you wanna, like, go out sometime for not sushi?" he blurted, facing her. She peeled away from the stars to look at him, but the constellations were still dancing in front of her. "Or just go out in general?" he asked.

Her heart skipped a beat and then started up again with the oomph of a drumming circle on Hippie Hill in Golden Gate Park. "Like, as more than friends?" Nat asked.

"Yeah," he said.

Suddenly, his hand was back in her hand. Her heartbeat was in her fingers. The lyrics of the romantic Elphaba/Fiyero duet, "As Long As You're Mine," rang out in her head.

"So, do you wanna dance?" he asked.

"Definitely." Nat transferred back into her chair and put her right hand in his. Her fingers clasping his fingers, she rolled back and forth. Then Malik twirled himself. "I guess that works," she said, giggling.

"Anything works!" He bumped his eyebrows mischievously. "Try something."

Nat tried to think over her tugging heartstrings, but when her mind came up blank, her arms stepped in. She grabbed Malik's other hand. "Don't let go, 'kay?" She pulled herself in close, flung herself backward, and then bounced back into his arms.

"That's perfect! Yes!" Malik fell to his knees, and his outstretched arms met Nat's waist. "I wanted to slide to you, but, you know, splinters."

Nat exploded with giggles, throwing her arms over his shoulders. They swayed for a few seconds like that—Malik on his knees, their eyes level. No guy had ever touched her waist. The image of it unleashed tingles all over her face.

He cocked his chin a little to the side. She cocked hers, too. But to the same side. *Ahh!* She wished she'd had practice. She wished Calvin hadn't cut their stage kiss. She wished Hudson had directed that they add it back in—but just the Elphaba/Fiyero kiss, not the Glinda/Fiyero one. *Try to keep it cool,* Nat told herself as *Popstar!*'s first-kiss stories cartwheeled through her brain, making her dizzy.

Malik paused to look into her eyes. His had little flecks of caramel in them, she just noticed. "You okay?" he asked.

"Yeah, totally, are you?"

"Uh-huh."

They leaned in at the same time, slowly, until his warm lips met hers. Everything but his breath was pushed out of focus. It was sweet like icing. Time was warped. Nat thought she could stay this way for forever, or at least until her lungs gave out.

"I'll make every last moment last."

"Are you hearing that?" he asked, gently pulling away, their noses brushing.

"What?" Nat turned her head toward the sliding glass door, where Rey was serenading them with the *Wicked* song from her phone. Meeting eyes, Rey stumbled backward into Hudson, and their pounding footsteps and giggles receded to the living room.

Nat and Malik looked at each other and burst out laughing. "Aw, man," he said. "For some reason, I thought that song was playing in my head."

"Me too! What?!"

"Wow, we're dorks."

They laughed some more, and then Malik scooted close, and Nat let her head fall onto his shoulder. They stayed like that for what felt like an entire cast album.

"So," he finally said, softly, "you ready for tomorrow's show?"

She was. Giddily ready. "I can't believe we get to do this all over again."

"I get so sad after a run of a show. I cry."

"You do?"

"Yup. But then I remember there's always next summer."

Nat smiled. "Do you think Broadway Bounders will be back in business?"

"Definitely. And if not, I think we can handle it, don't you?"

"For sure." She clapped her hands on his shoulders. "What show do you think we'll do?"

"Maybe *West Side Story* or *The Pajama Game*?"

"Ooh! Maybe we can do *Seussical* or . . . Wait for it . . . *Hamilton*!"

"We'd never get the rights."

"Never."

"But, hey, when I'm Burr to your Ham on Broadway, we'll get to do it eight times a week. How wild is that?"

Nat didn't let Malik's assumption blow past her. *When* they'd be on Broadway. Not if. He saw who she truly was. Her chair was a part of her, a special part of her, but it didn't define her. "Wild," she replied quietly.

"Sorry to interrupt," Fig said suddenly, opening the sliding door. He'd inadvertently let Warbucks out, and he was spinning around in circles on the deck, chasing his tail. He'd definitely gotten to the cake. "Nat, your parents are in the living room. All our parents have been texting. It's time to scat."

Malik pulled his phone from his pocket and it was lit up with messages. "Yikes . . . My dad's been sitting in the driveway for ten minutes."

"Oh no, sorry to—"

"Worth it," he cut in, his eyes shining as he jumped up from the bench.

She transferred into her chair and led Malik through the yard toward the front of the house, stopping at the side garden. She wasn't about to let her parents come between their goodbye.

"Wanna trade show posters tomorrow before call time?" Malik asked, hedging against a honeysuckle bush. "Write longer messages to each other on the back?"

"That's such a Fiyero thing to do," she said, poking fun at him.

"Well, that's such an Elphie thing to *say*," he said, poking fun right back.

She grinned a *Yes, of course they could trade*, and he kissed her cheek. The warmth of it shot down to her belly, breaking free an ensemble of butterflies from their cocoons. They spread their wings, wider, wider, fluttering against her insides, lifting her from her chair.

"Cool, cool, see ya tomorrow," he said.

"Yup, tomorrow," she said back.

No one puts Natty in a corner!
NO ONE! Your biggest fan,
Hudson

You always strive for good, just
like Elphaba. Love, Nicole

Your singing moves me to
smiles! Till next summer,
Marti

Hey, what happens in
Oz stays in Oz. —Fig

See, I did do a better job at Doctor
Dillamond than Fig! Baaaa, Kyle

From frenemy to friend, you've changed me
for the better. Hearts, Savannah Alexis

You make me wanna dance
through life. Elmo, Mop,
Normal, Yours, Malik

From one wicked witch to another,
I gotta say: Lookin' fly, sistah!
—Rey

You're water buckets
of fun! xo, Gia

**I want to be like you when I grow
up. Seriously, Kyra**

Blocking is the choreography of
acting. I know that now. —Petey

We should do Bat Boy next
summer and you should be Shelley!
—Leeza

The coolest cat bound for
Broadway! Peace, Avi

Everything is legal in New Jersey.
(A Hamilton quote cuz he duels and dies here)
—Aiden

Green suits you!
—Jayden

**You gave my mom
chills. —Steven**

A talkback with authors Stacy and Ali

STACY: Ali! The first time I saw you, I was sitting in the audience, weeping over the Deaf West production of *Spring Awakening* on Broadway. I remember watching you play Anna and thinking, *Wow! That girl can sing. That girl can act. That girl can dance*. When I knew I wanted to write what would become *The Chance to Fly*, all I could think about was *I need to meet Ali!*

ALI: Yes!!! I remember we met at Westville in Chelsea on Valentine's Day in 2017 and we instantly clicked. We bonded over our love for theater, specifically *Annie*.

STACY: Yuuup. I told you that my first introduction to theater was a production of *Annie* in a community theater in Merrick, Long Island. I was a shy kid, but when I played the tough orphan, Pepper, I came alive. Playing a role that was so far from who I was freed me up offstage—I made instant connections with my new theater family and became a clowny, upbeat, offbeat, dream-hard kid. I went on to perform in SIX MORE productions of *Annie*!

ALI: That's a lot of *Annie*.

STACY: Yes.

ALI: Coincidentally, my first show was *Annie*, too! I was seven, and it was a backyard production. My dad played Miss Hannigan, the evil woman who runs the orphanage, and I was Annie! So we talked about all that, and I remember I was just getting into writing. I showed you a scene I'd written about being thirteen and slow dancing with a crush.

STACY: Yes! It was so sweet! Because of that scene, we made sure we got that moment in for Nat. In the last chapter, she *finally* gets to slow dance with Malik! Aw! And I remember sharing with you my first book in the Camp Rolling Hills series to give you a sample of my work for middle-grade readers.

ALI: Soooo good! You then pitched me your idea about a new theater book featuring a character in a wheelchair, and I was sold.

STACY: I remember you were like, "I want to write it with you," and my jaw dropped. I don't know if I screamed "Yes!" but I was definitely screaming it on the inside. I was honored, you know. In front of me was this groundbreaking actress who'd just agreed to a collaboration.

ALI: Ha! I felt the same! It was pretty wild.

STACY: Anyway, we agreed to do this project together, and I think what made it work so well was that it was all about yes-anding each other and really listening to each other's feedback.

ALI: Yes, AND . . . we had similar goals with the project, which helped, too. So much of Nat's experiences are modeled after my own experiences. Growing up in a wheelchair and pursuing acting, I had a lot of firsts during theater productions. My first sleepover, my first crush, and my first kiss all came out of shows! I learned so much about who I was and the way in which I could move in my body. But also, like Nat, I didn't see myself represented in shows, television, movies, or books I was exposed to.

STACY: Nat uses a wheelchair, but it was also really important for us to tackle the broader theme of representation in the book—specifically in theater. Nat and Hudson bond over the idea that casting can be flexible. That actors can try on different roles and show the world that there's more to them than what people initially see.

ALI: When Nat goes to audition for *Wicked*, she believes Nessarose is the perfect character for her because she's also in a wheelchair. By the time she's cast as Elphaba, a typically able-bodied role, Nat realizes that her type is more than just the character in a wheelchair. She is capable of playing ANY role. I never imagined myself playing a role in *Oklahoma!* on Broadway because, it being a traditional show, I thought it would be cast traditionally. But I learned that the world is ready to see and celebrate someone like me onstage.

We also wanted Nat's conflict to not just be centered on her disability. Instead, we made it a priority to focus on Nat's coming-of-age story: finding her group, finding her voice, proving her independence to her parents, and learning she could fulfill her dreams beyond what she'd ever imagined.

STACY: We wanted this story to resonate with all kids who face challenges: Kids who feel lost. Kids who are still learning who they are. Kids who haven't found their group. But also, we wanted the story to resonate with theater-lovers and non-theater-lovers alike!

Writing Nat's story absolutely brought me back to my childhood, when auditioning made my stomach flip and opening nights gave me the butterfly-iest butterflies. The Oz Bounderz are just like the theater friends I grew up with, and it was a blast hanging out with them.

ALI: They feel like my friends, too! I love Hudson, especially.

STACY: I once tried to text Hudson, and then I stopped myself and was like, *We made him up!*

ALI: Hahaha. I love that scene with Hudson trying out Nat's chair.

STACY: Me too.

ALI: There's so much fear surrounding disability, and that chapter in particular is one where we really flip that on its head. Disability doesn't have to come with limitations. In fact, with the right support system, limitations can become an opportunity. That's my mantra!

STACY: No matter who you are and what challenges you face, remember: Creativity is key. You can break boundaries. You can burst through boxes.

ALI: You can defy gravity. Not to be too on the nose.

STACY: It's PERFECTLY on the nose!

ALI: Okay, fine!

ALI and STACY: Thank you for reading!

Stacy's Acknowledgments

On Valentine's Day of 2017, I met Ali Stroker and totally fangirled. We exchanged chocolate and stories and decided right then and there to create a brainchild together. Thus, *The Chance to Fly* was born. I took a stab at the first chapter, with the opening words being "I FOUND OKLAHOMA!" and Ali called to tell me that she'd just been cast in *Oklahoma!* at St. Ann's Warehouse in Brooklyn. Eventually, the announcement of Abrams's acquisition of *Chance* went public, and two days later, Ali went on to win the Tony for her role in the Broadway production. *Kismet.* This project has been an absolute dream. Ali and I got to write about the joys and magic of musical theater and how transformative it can be for kids, especially those who've yet to shine and find their group. Plus, Ali's simply the most wonderful collaborator.

A big, beautiful thank you to all the places I found my group, my best friends, my people. Calhoun High School's On Tour Company under the direction of Sal Salerno, where drama was my entire world alongside forever friends: Nicole, Matt, Amanda, Corey, Jon, Dan, Kris, Elissa, Ilissa, Jenga, Marti, and Jared. *Poo-wa-bah!*

A dramatic thank you to my fellow Columbia University School of the Arts' Acting Class of Dimes, who tolerated my musicalization of every classic play. Shakespearean shout-outs to Meera, Jason, Justin, Brent, Anjili, and Elizabeth.

A Jumbo thank you to 3Ps (Pen, Paint, and Pretzels) and Torn Ticket II, the student-run theater organizations at Tufts University, where my very first play went up onstage, where I had the opportunity to perform dream roles, and where I instantly found my family. Shout-out to Brian, David, Katie, Molly, Caitlin, Dana, Laura, Joél, Dave, Luke, Armen, Telly, Dan, Ashley, Julia, Mo, and of course, my longtime bestie and editor, Erica Finkel.

Sing her name: *Erica Finkel!* When we met doing the freshman show of *Clue*, where I was the Singing Telegram Girl to your Mrs. Peacock, I could never have imagined that we'd collaborate so closely for another eighteen-plus years. From 41 Ossipee to Camp Rolling Hills to being bridesmaids at each other's weddings, it feels perfect that you've sculpted this story. I mean, you sang "Defying Gravity" at your senior recital, and I sang "For Good" at mine, and as conjoined twins sharing a T-shirt, we sang the duet "Who Will Love Me as I Am?" Who else would I want as my editor on this book?! You're a visionary.

Mom and Dad, thank you for introducing me to theater. For nurturing and supporting my passion with singing lessons, recordings, schooling, and rides to auditions, play rehearsals, and shows my entire childhood. Dad, thanks for being my biggest fan and mouthing along to every song I have ever sung onstage. Mom, when our elementary school didn't offer a theater program, you went on to direct and choreograph the musical. Thanks for unbiasedly casting me as Annie!

To my sister, Amy, and my brother, Mike, with whom I've performed in countless community theater and camp shows, thanks for humoring me with our living room productions. I took them very seriously, and I appreciate you tolerating my theater dictatorship.

Grandma Terry, thank you for saving and/or framing every theater program of mine, for taking me to two Broadway shows a year, and for somehow convincing Brooke Shields to call me up to bow with the cast of *Grease* because it was my "birthday." (It wasn't.) Grandma Joanie, thank you for collecting my plays and books, gifting them to your friends, and being unabashedly honest about which ones you like best. Grandpa Lenny, the world's most gorgeous cantor, thanks for always singing your heart out and for encouraging me to do the same.

To my brave students at Uptown Stories, Naked Angels, and Oxbridge, thank you for inspiring me every day with your lack of inhibition. You keep my imagination fed.

Alec Strum, thank you for introducing me to Ali and for making this dream project come to life. Without you, there would be no *Chance*!

Jazz hands for Hannah Mann, our literary agent at Writers House. Thank you for your relentless support. Without you, Ali and I wouldn't have had the guts to write this book. You're patient, kind, honest, cool, and fast. We feel endlessly lucky to be working with you.

To my Creative Artists Agency fam: Thank you to Dana Spector and Berni Barta, my film and television agents for *Chance*; and Ally Shuster, my theatrical literary agent, who's always such a fierce advocate of my plays. Disney, Ali and I can't wait.

Erica Finkel (again and again) and the whole brilliant team at Abrams, especially Marie Oishi, Marcie Lawrence, Kathy Lovisolo, Andrew Smith, Jody Mosley, Michael Jacobs, Melanie Chang, Trish McNamara, Jenny Choy, Nicole Schaefer, Hallie Patterson, Brooke Shearouse, Kim Lauber, Elisa Gonzalez, Wendy Ceballos, and Emily Daluga. Ali and I thank you for helping this story reach all the theater nerds and non-theater nerds alike. Everyone deserves the chance to fly.

My Fiyero, Tim Borecky, thank you for lending me your wisdom and dramaturgy every time I cornered you to read you chapters. I appreciate your indulging my characters as if they were our friends. I love that you're a musical theater lover.

To my twin boys, Benji and Jet, I wrote this book while I was pregnant with you. Every kick was a tap dance, every hiccup a song. I love watching you grow and am so grateful for your love of music.

To all the theater people out there, keep belting your heart out.

Ali's Acknowledgments

First, I want to thank my wonderful collaborator, Stacy. Without her, this book would not exist. Our theater nerd hearts clicked the moment we met, and I knew we would create something beautiful together. I had no idea how creative, supportive, and exciting this process would be. I am so grateful for your work ethic, your imagination, and your ability to listen. Thank you for wanting to write this book with me.

A huge thank-you to all the teachers and angels who believed in me when I was growing up, wanting to pursue theater with every fiber of my being. Kim Galbreith, Susan McBrayer, Noreen Clark, and Laurie Sales: You saw something burning inside me that needed to be expressed, and you gave me so many chances to do it.

Mom and Dad: You both have been my cheerleaders, my guides, and my light. You drove me to NYC for auditions and rehearsals, ran lines with me, and listened to hours and hours of me singing in the house. Under not-so-normal circumstances, you helped me achieve my dreams in the most spectacular ways. Thank you forever. Tory, Jake, Dan, Alissa, JP, and LD—my siblings, my nephews—thank you for showing up at my performances, for calling to wish me good luck, and for always supporting my career. I am the luckiest.

My friends, you know who you are. You have picked me up when I didn't know if I could keep going. You have helped me process my successes and failures. You have showed up with love and support.

My team, Ted, Rachel, Jed, KMR, Ira, Julie, Hannah, Erica: Thank you for working so hard to help me achieve my goals and dreams. Thank you for your support and authenticity and belief in me.

David, my love. My entire life. Thank you for helping me be my most authentic self as an artist and human being in this world. From the moment you walked into my life, you have been the most supportive, collaborative, and selfless partner. Thank you for choosing me every day. I love you more than anything.

About the Authors

Ali Stroker won the 2019 Tony Award for Best Performance by a Featured Actress in a Musical for her role as Ado Annie in Rodgers and Hammerstein's *Oklahoma!* She made history as the first actor in a wheelchair to appear on Broadway when she originated the role of Anna in Deaf West's revival of *Spring Awakening*. Ali is also the first actress in a wheelchair to graduate from NYU's Tisch drama program. Ali has appeared on *The Glee Project*, *Glee*, *Ten Days in the Valley*, *Lethal Weapon*, *Instinct*, and *Drunk History*. In addition to her performing, Ali has been a cochair of Women Who Care, which supports United Cerebral Palsy of NYC. She cofounded Be More Heroic, an anti-bullying campaign. In addition, she has led theater workshops for South African women and children affected by HIV and AIDS. Ali's dedication to improving lives through the arts, disabled or not, is captured in her motto: "Making Your Limitations Your Opportunities." Ali is a founding member of TAG Theater Company and lives in New York City with her boyfriend, David. alistroker.com.

Stacy Davidowitz is the author of the Camp Rolling Hills series and coauthor of *Camp Rolling Hills the Musical*, which continues to have productions across the country. She is also the author of the Hanazuki chapter-book series based on Hasbro's YouTube series. Stacy has written award-winning plays that have been produced regionally and internationally and are published by Broadway Play Publishing, Stage Rights, and YouthPLAYS. When she is not writing, she teaches creative writing and musical theater in schools, foster care facilities, and juvenile detention centers. She is a proud graduate of Tufts University and Columbia University, where she earned degrees in drama and acting. Fun fact: Growing up, she was in seven productions of *Annie.* Stacy lives in Manhattan with her husband and twin boys. stacydavidowitz.com.